SUPERNATURAL™

John Winchester's Journal

Also by Alex Irvine

The *Supernatural* Book of Monsters,
Spirits, Demons, and Ghouls

A Scattering of Jades

One King, One Soldier

Unintended Consequences

Isaac Asimov's Have Robot, Will Travel

The Narrows

Batman: Inferno

The Life of Riley

Pictures from an Expedition

The Ultimates: Against All Enemies

SUPERNATURAL™

John Winchester's Journal

Alex Irvine

Illustrations by Dan Panosian and Alex Irvine

Supernatural™ created by Eric Kripke

ωm

WILLIAM MORROW

An Imprint of HarperCollins*Publishers*

FIRST EDITION

Designed by Timothy Shaner, NightandDayDesign.biz

Library of Congress Cataloging-in-Publication Data
Irvine, Alexander (Alexander C.)
  Supernatural : John Winchester's journal / Alex Irvine. — 1st ed.
      p. cm.
  "Supernatural created by Eric Kripke."
  Prequel to the CW TV show Supernatural.
  ISBN 978-0-06-170662-2
  1. Supernatural—Fiction. I. Supernatural (Television program : 2005–)
II. Title.
  PS3609.R85S87 2009
  813'.6—dc22   2008049967

09 10 11 12 13   OV/RRD   10 9 8 7 6 5 4 3 2 1

SUPERNATURAL™

John Winchester's Journal

1983

November 16:

I went to Missouri, and learned the truth. And from her, I met Fletcher Gable, who gave me this book and said: "Write everything down." That's what Fletcher told me, like this new life is a school and I'll flunk out if I don't have good notes. Only if I flunk out of this school, I'll be dead. And the boys will be orphans. So I'm going to go back to where this started.

Two weeks ago, my wife was murdered. I watched her die, pinned to the ceiling of Sammy's room, blood dripping onto his cradle until she burst into flames—looking at me as she died. The week before that, we were a normal family . . . eating dinner, going to Dean's T-ball game, buying toys for baby Sammy. But in an instant, it all changed . . . When I try to think back, get it straight in my head . . . I feel like I'm going crazy. Like someone ripped both my arms off, plucked my eyes out . . . I'm wandering around, alone and lost, and I can't do anything.

Mary used to write books like this one. She said it helped her remember all the little things, about the boys, me . . . I wish I could read her journals, but like everything else, they're gone. Burned into nothing. She always wanted me to try writing things down. Maybe she was right, maybe it will help me to remember, to understand. Fletcher seems to think so.

Nothing makes any sense anymore . . . My wife is gone,

my sons are without their mother . . . the things I saw that night, I remember hearing Mary scream, and I ran, but then . . . everything was calm, just for a second—Sammy was fine—and I was sure I had been hearing things—too many horror movies too late at night. But then there was the blood, and when I looked up, my wife . . .

Half our house is gone, even though the fire burned for only a few hours. Most of our clothes and photos are ruined, even our safe—the safe with Mary's old diaries, the passbooks for the boys' college accounts, what little jewelry we had . . . all gone. How could my house, my whole life, go up like that, so fast, so hot? How could my wife just burn up and disappear?

I want my wife back. Oh God, I want her back.

I thought at first that we would stay. Mike and Kate helped me take care of the boys at first, and Julie's been great too, but I tried to tell them—tell Mike—what I think happened that night. He just looked at me, this look . . . like he's sure I'm crazy. He must have told Kate something too. Out of no-where she said the next morning, I should think about seeing a shrink. How can I talk to a stranger about this? I never saw a shrink for everything I went through in the Marines, and I got through that. My friends think I'm going insane. Who knows, maybe I am . . .

The police quit on the case as soon as they couldn't pin it on me. They don't care that she was on the ceiling, they don't care about the blood on her stomach or about any of the things I've seen since then. They want a tidy answer. Doesn't matter to them whether it's the right one. The last time I talked to them, a week after she died, they asked me the same questions they asked me the night of the fire. Where was I? How was my relationship with Mary in the weeks prior to the fire? Any problems with the boys? I can tell where they're going.

Mary's uncle Jacob had a funeral for her in Illinois, where

she was from. I didn't go. Why? There was nothing to bury, and I don't think I could have listened to what anyone there would have said. I've been drinking too much, trailing off in the middle of sentences. I hear things at night while I sit in Sam and Dean's room. Everything lately feels like those instances when you remember a dream a few days after you had it, but then you can't remember if it was a dream or if it actually happened. I keep going over that night in my head . . . why did I ever get out of bed? I left my wife by herself to go watch TV, and she died. I'm so sorry, Mary.

Dean still hardly talks. I try to make small talk, or ask him if he wants to throw the baseball around. Anything to make him feel like a normal kid again. He never budges from my side—or from his brother. Every morning when I wake up, Dean is inside the crib, arms wrapped around baby Sam. Like he's trying to protect him from whatever is out there in the night.

Sammy cries a lot, wanting his mom. I don't know how to stop it, and part of me doesn't want to. It breaks my heart to think that soon he won't remember her at all. I can't let her memory die.

Woke up yesterday morning with a nasty hangover . . . Wasn't in the mood to do much of anything, much less have a heart-to-heart with Mike, who jumped on me the second I walked into the kitchen. I guess that's his right, since it was his house. He was going on about how I have to get myself together, for the boys . . . but he seemed more concerned about the garage than anything else. Accusing me of phoning it in, you've barely been in to work . . . No kidding I've barely been in to work . . . My wife is dead, something horrible happened to her, maybe my boys are at risk too . . . how can I forget about all that and go to work, for God's sake?

Anyway, I told him he could have it. That stopped him

3

cold. "You're telling me you're gonna give up your life's work over this?" Watch me, Mike. It's yours.

I walked out of the house with Mike's check in my hand. He wasn't so worried about me that he wouldn't let me go. Do I blame him? I don't know. I took the boys back to Julie's and went to the first check-cashing place I could find. Walked out with enough cash to fill the back of the car with security. Two 12-gauges—Winchester 1300 pump and a Stevens 311 side-by-side. Spread of sidearms—good old Browning 9 mm, .44 Desert Eagle, snub Ruger SP101, and a little pocket .22. That'll do for a start.

Haven't ever written anything this long in my life. Hope I never do again.

Went to see Missouri for the second time, and I can't explain it . . . it was like we'd been friends for years. She knew every detail, not just of my life, but also of me . . . my thoughts . . . fears. She was the first person who didn't look at me like I was crazy when I told her my story . . . she just listened, and nodded, and then she told me she believed me.

She also said that if I wanted answers, I'd need to make a sacrifice. A blood sacrifice. So I pulled out one of my own fingernails, like I did that every day. She had a vision, and we found a bloody mess in a neighbor's house along with the words WE'RE COMING FOR THE CHILDREN written in blood. I don't remember anything between that and finding Sam and Dean safe back at Julie's, thank God, but Julie . . . Julie was dead. Something just tore her apart. Missouri found a tooth in her body, I tried to draw it but I can't draw. I took the boys, said good-bye to Missouri, and got the hell out of Lawrence. If I never go back, it'll be too soon.

Not for Dean, though. The first thing he wanted to know was when we would go home. But we don't have a home anymore, Dean. The sooner you get used to that, the better. We don't have a home until we find what killed your mother.

First stop, Eureka. Fletcher said we should start there.

November 19:

I'm going to try to write this down just as it happened, no matter how unbelievable. Because if I can't believe it myself—if I can't rationally write down what I saw—how is anyone else ever going to believe it?

Jacob showed up looking for the boys. I talked him into coming with me to a cemetery where I thought there might be some answers, and I got him killed. The hellhound—that's what Fletcher calls it—came out of a crypt and it tore holes in him like I haven't seen in a human being since Vietnam. Then H was there. I don't know who he is, but he saved my life like I couldn't save Jacob's. But he wouldn't let me take Jacob to a hospital. He said Jacob was dying, and that whatever we were looking for, it was keeping him alive to prolong his suffering. I didn't want to believe him, but he'd been right about what happened up until then . . . There was nothing we could do, H said, and God help me I went along with him, and I stood there and watched while my car rolled into a quarry with Jacob dying inside.

And all H said was, "Guess you got a new car." That cold-blooded bastard. I may learn from him, but I'll never like him, and I'll never trust him. He started talking about demons. Hellhounds, demons . . .

I let Jacob die. Could I have saved him? Maybe not, maybe H was right. But I didn't even try. What am I becoming? I always tried to conduct myself so that if the boys asked me why I did something, I wouldn't have to lie to them. But what am I going to say if they ever ask me about their uncle Jake?

November 20:

I killed a man in cold blood tonight.

No. I killed a shapeshifting monster tonight to protect all of the people who don't know things like that exist. But it would have looked like a man to any of those people. And Dean saw it happen.

It looked like Ichi, a hunter H took me out with. We were

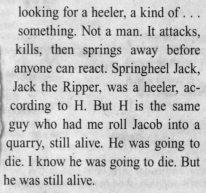

looking for a heeler, a kind of . . . something. Not a man. It attacks, kills, then springs away before anyone can react. Springheel Jack, Jack the Ripper, was a heeler, according to H. But H is the same guy who had me roll Jacob into a quarry, still alive. He was going to die. I know he was going to die. But he was still alive.

And then tonight, Dean walked out of the roadhouse right when I put the final bullet into the shape-shifter's head. And he said, Why'd you kill him, Dad?

How am I supposed to answer that? Because he wasn't a man, he was a monster who looked like a man? My boy walked out the door and saw me shoot someone in the head. Maybe I'm the monster who looks like a man.

Back up. Write everything down.

H said he was going to start showing me the ropes. There are people who hunt monsters. They have a kind of network, moving through places like Bill and Ellen's roadhouse. Bill is a hunter, and they have a little girl, Jo. She's not much older than Sammy. The hunters swap stories about what they've seen. They're all damaged, broken. They hate the things they hunt. I'm just like them.

Ellen's niece watched the boys while H took me and Ichi

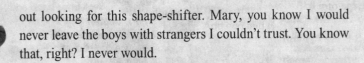

out looking for this shape-shifter. Mary, you know I would never leave the boys with strangers I couldn't trust. You know that, right? I never would.

November 21:

The boys are with Pam and Bill in Elgin. I haven't spent a whole night away from them since Mary died, and I can feel it like a hook in my gut, wanting to get back to them, protect them. But H says I need to talk to Mary again, and if he can make that happen . . .

He goes on about demons. A demon killed his wife, he says, and just expects me to believe it. But what he looks like to me is someone who let grief turn him into a monster. Whatever happened to his wife, it doesn't excuse what he's done. And I can't let myself turn into him. I'm not a hunter. I'm a husband and father who wants revenge for his wife.

Here's what I wish I could say to Dean—Your brother's too young to understand any of this, but you're beginning to. And that scares me. Since your mother died, I've seen unspeakable things, and now you've seen them and that's my fault. I feel the darkness of the road I'm traveling on now. It's not a place for you. One day you'll see—I had to leave you today . . . but when I'm done, I promise you: the day will come when I never have to leave you again. Until then, I can only pray that you're strong enough to look after Sam. One of us has to be.

November 24:

We're on the way to somewhere, H and me, but I'm the rookie and I don't get to ask where. He says he's taking me to meet someone who's going to let me talk to Mary, but before that we need to do a couple of things.

A hunter never passes up a hunt.

Never.

This is what H says. So tonight we took on a strange kind of undead thing. H said it was a revenant, maybe? I don't know what that is. Yet. I'll find out.

People called it Doc Benton. He wanted to live forever, and when he couldn't make alchemy work, he turned to organ theft instead. He kept himself alive by replacing each of his organs, as they failed one at a time, with organs harvested from unlucky locals. According to H, this has been going on since 1816. The doc was trouble, until I took him apart with a chainsaw after H burned the corpse of his most recent victim.

Lesson: burning the victim weakened the doc by depriving him of the power he'd gotten from those organs. According to H, you can solve a lot of problems with gasoline and a match.

I need to learn more about revenants. I need to learn more about everything.

November 25:

Today, in a town called Blue Earth, Minnesota, I met a crazy priest who brought Mary to me. His name is Jim, but what he did wasn't like any church ritual I've ever seen, and I doubt he learned it in a seminary. He cut himself, and his blood turned into fire, but it didn't burn him. And then the fire turned into Mary.

Mary.

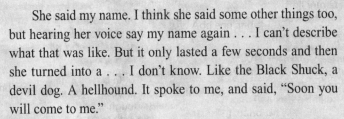

She said my name. I think she said some other things too, but hearing her voice say my name again . . . I can't describe what that was like. But it only lasted a few seconds and then she turned into a . . . I don't know. Like the Black Shuck, a devil dog. A hellhound. It spoke to me, and said, "Soon you will come to me."

After it was gone, Jim looked at the hellhound's tooth. There are numbers on it: 1127. Mary died at 11:27, according to the police report. H and Jim agreed that the numbers were some kind of coordinate carved into the tooth, but what does it mean?

Written in blood: In olden times in the West people used to say "I put my hand and seal" on a document when signing it. In the East this was literal in some cases. The emperor of Japan in ancient days "signed" important documents by dipping his hand in blood and putting a full bloody handprint on the page. In the history of pacts with the Devil, people were supposed to sign their names in blood. I have seen a couple of alleged pacts from earlier centuries and neither, as far as I can tell, was signed in blood, though they do bear signatures of people. Blood undoubtedly stressed the seriousness of the signing. You were giving away your soul. "The Blood Is the Life."

November 27:

1,700 miles in 24 hours flat, me and H handing the wheel back and forth, from Blue Earth to Tempe. Fletcher Gable. He showed us a map of cemeteries—Devil's Gates, he called them. Places where demons can get through to our world. I don't know about demons, but the map was divided into sectors, and cemetery #112 in Zone 7 was in Hope, Colorado, near the Four Corners.

I don't know how to explain what happened there. The Fore Inn, set on the edge of a town full of dead bodies, hallucinations . . . we found the inn, and there was the hellhound, the Black Shuck, and it came to H like a spaniel. He said he didn't kill Mary, but he set the dog on me, and said he knew "some of the players involved." But they weren't demons, he said. I killed the dog, and then H changed his whole tack. Said that everything he'd done, even siccing the dog on me, was a way to get me to hunt. He said he wasn't H, he was something else in a hunter's body. A man's body. All I could think of was shooting the shape-shifter outside the roadhouse with Dean as a witness. I killed H, and I burned the hotel. I'm writing this at a rest stop on I-76 outside Julesburg. I killed H, and I'll goddamn well hunt, all right. I'll hunt, and the boys will hunt, and we will find whatever killed Mary and we will send it to Hell. And on the way, we will kill every monster and ghoul and ghost and demon and anything else. My boys will not grow up to experience what I have. They will not lose what I have lost.

This black dog, or the divel in such a likenesse (God hee knoweth al who worketh all,) runing all along down the body of the church with great swiftnesse, and incredible haste, among the people, in a visible fourm and shape, passed between two persons, as they were kneeling uppon their knees, and occupied in prayer as it seemed, wrung the necks of them bothe

10

at one instant clene backward, in somuch that even at
a moment where they kneeled, they strangely dyed.

England, 1577. Scorch marks left on the
church door, known as Devil's Fingerprints.

November 29:

We're gone from Elgin. Where to, I don't know. Wherever I
can learn what happened to Mary, and kill whoever did it. The
hunters are out there. One of them must know something about
what happened to her. I'll head back to the roadhouse first. Bill
and Ellen will let us stay for a while. After that, who knows?

Never been much for books, but then I never was much for
keeping a journal, either. Things have changed. I started looking for old books like Fletcher has, like I saw some of the hunters reading at the roadhouse. I need to learn. Know your enemy.
And I started digging around libraries. I'm collecting old
police files, going through microfiche . . . looking for any fires,
arsons, with similar MOs to our fire. I'm gonna find this thing
that killed my wife, and when I do . . . God forgive me . . .

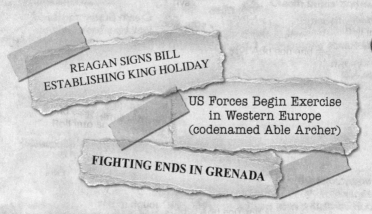

REAGAN SIGNS BILL
ESTABLISHING KING HOLIDAY

US Forces Begin Exercise
in Western Europe
(codenamed Able Archer)

FIGHTING ENDS IN GRENADA

December 11:

Sammy has finally started sleeping through the night, and now that Dean shares a bed with him, he's out like a light too. But me . . . I close my eyes and she's there. It always starts the same, I'm seeing her as she was before that night, beautiful and happy and alive. And I'm not seeing it, I'm living it, it's like I'm there . . . it's so real, I know I can reach out and touch her. And so I do . . . I reach out . . . and suddenly I'm back to that night, to the blood and the fire and Mary, Mary is on the ceiling, and how did she get on the ceiling . . . she can't be on the ceiling . . .

Here's the weird part. When I wake up, sweating and panting . . . I swear there is something there. I can feel it, hovering over me, over my boys. It's watching, it's waiting, I think it's even mocking me . . . You couldn't stop this. You couldn't keep her safe. You can't keep them safe.

December 14:

I actually fell asleep last night . . . then woke up in a cold sweat five minutes later. Feeling that presence again . . . and thinking. I've been reading about fires, how they start, how quickly they spread . . . but one of the books talked about strange fires, fires with no explanations . . . it said that some people believe fire can be controlled by certain evil entities, beings, and used to harm people. It's crazy, the stuff of fairy tales . . . like fire-breathing dragons, right? But then I remembered . . . when I went back into Sammy's room that night, when I tried to get to Mary . . . the fire leaped out. Leaped out at me . . . like it had a purpose, like it wanted to keep me away, to stop me from reaching her. Like someone was controlling it.

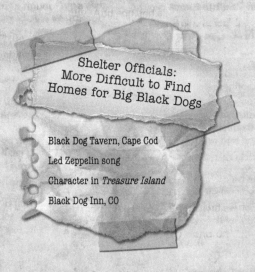

Shelter Officials:
More Difficult to Find
Homes for Big Black Dogs

Black Dog Tavern, Cape Cod

Led Zeppelin song

Character in *Treasure Island*

Black Dog Inn, CO

December 20:

I'm beginning to understand that there's nobody else but me. Other hunters have seen things. A guy named Frank Gutierrez told me with a straight face that Route 666 is thick with devil dogs. But every hunter's got a different story, and none of them have seen exactly what I've seen. If I want answers, I'm going to have to find them myself. Been reading about black dogs. Black Shuck. Old English *scucca* = demon. Also known as barghest, as a death omen.

Black dogs haunt roads. Sometimes they have a headless woman with them, or are headless. To see them means you will have a death in the family. Most of the written stories are British, but I've been asking around a little. Everybody's got a black dog story: in Macon County, Tennessee; Meriden, Connecticut; Long Island, Oregon.

December 25:

Didn't sleep again last night. Woke up in a cold sweat and realized it was Christmas. Where's Mary? That was my thought all night, and it stayed in my mind all day. Christmas without my wife seems unreal. Our celebration was clumsy . . . a crooked two-foot-tall plastic tree, a bunch of junk food stuffed in the stockings, and a pile of sports equipment for the boys . . . football, basketball, soccer ball. My attempt to bring back some normalcy. Already Dean is too big for T-ball, this year we'll be going to real Little League games. Or rather, I'll be going to the games. Alone.

Mary will never see Dean hit a home run. She'll never see Sammy walk, or hear him say his first words. She won't take Dean to his first day at school, or stay up all night with me worrying the first night he takes the car out. It's not right that she's not here, and that's all I could think about today. I'm so angry I can barely see straight—I want my wife back.

The police have officially declared our case closed. What a Christmas present, huh?

December 29:

Back at the roadhouse. We're going to stay here for a while. I can't just drive around in circles. The boys need a place they can think of as home, even if it doesn't last. And I need a place where I can learn what hunters do. The only holiday spirit I have is bloodlust. I want to kill. The last time I remember feeling like this was Vietnam. But I think we can stay here for a while to get our feet on the ground. Or I can get my feet on the ground, anyway; I don't know what it will take for the boys to feel normal again. Dean hasn't been the same since he saw me kill that shape-shifter. I don't know how to talk to him about it. He's not even five years old. Most kids his age don't even have a clear idea what death is, and he's seen it up close and personal. What do I say to him? How old does he have to be before I tell him the truth?

1984

January 1:

Today a new year begins. Mary loved this time of year; she loved the idea of a fresh start for everyone. She always made a resolution, one a year, and unlike most people, she kept hers. And every year she tried to talk me into making one, but I could never see the point. I wish I could have seen her diary. Maybe it would help me remember her. Maybe it would clue me in to some of her secrets. Maybe that's the point of a diary. Keep your stories, your life, from dying. So that other people don't forget.

God I wish the boys could have known Mary longer.

This year I'm finally making a resolution. I'm going to find out what happened to my wife.

January 24:

Dean turns five today. I was thinking about where we're going to be in the fall, because he should start school. Then I realized that I can't leave him in a school. Anything could happen. Maybe a place that has half-day kindergarten. Maybe that I could do. I know I should. I know he should be able to run around with other kids, who don't know how to field-strip the Browning. Well, Dean doesn't either, yet. But he's learning. He's got a talent for guns. I can see it already. And he'll need it.

May 2:

Sammy is a year old. We spent his birthday in the mountains, because I had to meet a guy named Daniel Elkins. The hunter culture is weird about how it breaks in new blood. Everyone you meet says you should go meet someone else, and learn something else, and every time you meet someone else they take you out to hunt their favorite kind of monster. This guy Elkins lives in a cabin out in the middle of nowhere in Colorado, and according to him, he's the greatest vampire hunter alive.

Vampires.

They're real. I've never seen one, but Daniel says they're real, and I believe him. He also says that the hunter's journal is for research as much as for recording day-to-day whatever. So I copied this from a book called the *Harleian Miscellany*:

> *We must not omit Observing here, that our Landlord seems to pay some regard to what Baron Valvasor has related of the Vampyres, said to infest some Parts of this Country. These Vampyres are supposed to be the Bodies of deceased Persons, animated by evil Spirits, which come out of the Graves, in the Night-time, suck the Blood of many of the Living, and thereby destroy them.*

Vampires, four hundred years ago. There are other records, even older. Peter Plogojewitz, the Shoemaker of Silesia . . .

May 17:

This would have been our sixth anniversary. Six is iron. Sammy took his first steps yesterday. He walked toward Dean, then fell flat on his face and started crying. Life is tough, kid. Do I sound like a proud dad? I am.

November 2:

Mary has been dead for a year. I'm never going to be over it, and I wouldn't want to be. But I've spent the last year getting better at revenge.

Maybe this is a good time to write down everything I've learned about Lawrence.

- Corner of 8th and Massachusetts: Ghost, woman in nineteenth-century dress.
- 7th and Massachusetts: Eldridge Hotel. Word is the city's going to rebuild it, so maybe the haunting will change—but Missouri says there's something about the fifth floor. She gets visions more easily there, like the spirit world is closer somehow.
- Stull Church: abandoned since 1922. No roof, but you can stand inside it in a thunderstorm and not get wet. Rain will not fall on it. A crucifix still hangs on the wall, and it turns upside down when you approach.
- Stull Cemetery: Devil said to appear there twice a year, on the vernal equinox and Halloween. He is visiting the grave of one of his children, born of a human witch and dead after a few days.
- Haskell Institute: children's cemetery near Taminend Hall, full of uneasy ghosts. Another ghost, a coed suicide, haunts the basement of Pocahontas Hall. Hiawatha Hall full of bad echoes, the sorrow and pain of generations of abused children. How many of them died?

I'm learning about hauntings. Everyone I've talked to and read thinks they know everything about hauntings, but they all say something different. Or so vague that it doesn't mean anything. I read this and that, and tell myself that if I keep doing it, I'll start to see the patterns.

> *In the world of spirits is always a very great number of them, as being the first sort of all, in order to their examination and preparation; but there is no fixed time for their stay; for some are translated to heaven and others confined to hell soon after their arrival; whilst some continue there for weeks, and others for several years . . . Ebenezer Sibly*

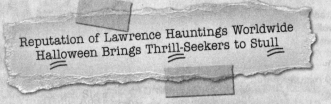

Reputation of Lawrence Hauntings Worldwide
Halloween Brings Thrill-Seekers to Stull

This reminded me of Doc Benton. From William of Newburgh:

> *As soon as this man was left alone in this place, the devil, imagining that he had found the right moment for breaking his courage, incontinently roused up his own chosen vessel, who appeared to have reposed longer than usual. Having beheld this from afar, he grew stiff with terror by reason of his being alone; but soon recovering his courage, and no place of refuge being at hand, he valiantly withstood the onset of the fiend, who came rushing upon him with a*

terrible noise, and he struck the axe which he wielded in his hand deep into his body. On receiving this wound, the monster groaned aloud, and turning his back, fled with a rapidity not at all inferior to that with which he had advanced, while the admirable man urged his flying foe from behind, and compelled him to seek his own tomb again; which opening of its own accord, and receiving its guest from the advance of the pursuer, immediately appeared to close again with the same facility. In the meantime, they who, impatient of the coldness of the night, had retreated to the fire ran up, though somewhat too late, and, having heard what had happened, rendered needful assistance in digging up and removing from the midst of the tomb the accursed corpse at the earliest dawn. When they had divested it of the clay cast forth with it, they found the huge wound it had received, and a great quantity of gore which had flowed from it in the sepulchre; and so having carried it away beyond the walls of the monastery and burnt it, they scattered the ashes to the winds.

Everyone agrees that you have to burn them to make sure they stay dead. Should have burned Doc Benton, too, but I'm guessing the chainsaw did the trick.

1985

January 1:

New Year's Day. Mary, I promised last year that I would avenge you. I promise again. I'll promise it every year until it happens. I'll never forget.

January 24:

Dean's sixth birthday. It's been more than a year since he saw me kill a shape-shifter. He doesn't ask about it anymore. And he stopped asking when he's going to go to school. I tried to do it last fall, but I couldn't. I just couldn't risk it. Maybe this year, now that he's a little older, now that he knows a little more about things. I've been teaching him. Not the worst stuff, but enough so he knows that there are things that go bump in the night.

Myling. Scandinavian child spirit, also called utburd. Typically the souls of murdered children, or children who died unbaptized. They will ride travelers at night and demand to be taken to a graveyard so they can rest, but they get heavier and heavier as the graveyard gets closer, until the person carrying them is driven under the earth by their weight. This belief is derived from the practice of leaving unwanted or deformed infants out to die of exposure. Generally they haunt the location where they were abandoned, but folklore also notes their presence in the dwellings of those who killed them—usually a family member. If their remains can be located and buried in hallowed ground, they will disappear.

May 2:

Sammy is two today. Two years in a row we've spent his birthday in Colorado, where I had to stop by Daniel's. Still never seen a vampire, but Elkins is such a hermit that because I talk to him, other hunters are starting to ask me to pick his brain for them.

Crosses won't repel them, and sunlight won't kill them. They can go outside. They need blood to survive, and prefer human blood, but can survive on other mammals if there are no humans around. The only way to be sure of killing them is beheading—although the blood of a dead man is like poison to them. It won't kill them, but it weakens them, makes them slow and sick.

Daniel says they're extinct, but he keeps an eye out anyway, and he thinks I should know enough about them to take one on if there are any left. He gave me a copy of this article, in case it was ever useful.

. . . the body of the brother last dead was according exhumed, and "living" blood being found in the heart and in circulation, it was cremated, and the sufferer began immediately to mend and stood before me a hale, hearty and vigorous man of fifty years.

From American Anthropologist, 1896

May 17:

This would have been our seventh anniversary. Wool and copper.

There lived at Baghdad an aged merchant who had grown wealthy in his business, and who had an only son to whom he was tenderly attached. He resolved to marry him to the daughter of another merchant, a girl of considerable fortune, but without any personal attractions. Abul-Hassan, the merchant's son, on being shown the portrait of the lady, requested his father to delay the marriage till he could reconcile his mind to it. Instead, however, of doing this, he fell in love with another girl, the daughter of a sage, and he gave his father no peace till he consented to the marriage with the object of his affections. The old man stood out as long as he could, but finding that his son was bent on acquiring the hand of the fair Nadilla, and was equally resolute not to accept the rich and ugly lady, he did what most fathers, under such circumstances, are constrained to do, he acquiesced.

The wedding took place with great pomp and ceremony, and a happy honeymoon ensued, which might have been happier but for one little circumstance which led to very serious consequences.

Abul-Hassan noticed that his bride quitted the nuptial couch as soon as she thought her husband was asleep, and did not return to it, till an hour before dawn.

Filled with curiosity, Hassan one night feigned sleep, and saw his wife rise and leave the room as usual. He followed cautiously, and saw her enter a cemetery. By the straggling moonbeams he beheld her go into a tomb; he stepped in after her.

The scene within was horrible. A party of ghouls were assembled with the spoils of the graves they had violated, and were feasting on the flesh of the long-buried corpses. His own wife, who, by the way, never touched supper at home, played no inconsiderable part in the hideous banquet.

As soon as he could safely escape, Abul-Hassan stole back to his bed.

He said nothing to his bride till next evening when supper was laid and she declined to eat; then he insisted on her partaking, and when she positively refused, he exclaimed wrathfully, "Yes, you keep your appetite for your feast with the ghouls!" Nadilla was silent; she turned pale and trembled, and without a word sought her bed. At midnight she rose, fell on her husband with her nails and teeth, tore his throat, and having opened a vein, attempted to suck his blood; but Abul-Hassan springing to his feet threw her down, and with a blow killed her. She was buried the next day.

Three days after, at midnight, she reappeared, attacked her husband again, and again attempted to suck his blood. He fled from her, and on the morrow opened her tomb, burned her to ashes, and cast them into the Tigris.

MUTILATED DEAD COWS
FOUND ON HIGHWAY

Two Found Murdered in
Bizarre Suicide Pact

REAGAN TO ADDRESS CONGRESS TODAY

September 7:

Today was Dean's first day of school. I put him straight into first grade. He's almost seven, and I just told the school that he'd been in kindergarten back in Kansas. They didn't press too hard when I told them that the kids had lost their mother, and we'd been moving around. I think we'll stay here for a while. Or try, anyway. I felt normal again while I was taking Dean to school. He asked on the way in whether kids in school learned the same stuff he'd been learning. I had to tell him that maybe it wasn't a good idea for him to talk about Dad's job on the playground.

He came home on top of the world, and he brought me worksheets with the names of the different parts of a fish, different numbers of apples and oranges added together . . . this is what it should be like. Why can't it?

Sammy wants to be in school too. I can't even imagine staying in one place for long enough that he'll start here. Three years seems like forever.

November 2:

Mary has been dead for two years. I've been on the road for three days, cleaning up a haunted building in San Francisco. Already these are starting to seem like an everyday chore to me. You get the story, you find the remains, you burn them and salt them. End of story. These were two girls, and the whole ride back to the roadhouse I was thinking that I'll never have girls. Dean saw something on my face, or maybe it was just that he knew what day it is. When I got here, he came up to me and asked if I'd had a tough hunt. I couldn't talk for a minute.

November 14:

Took Dean shooting. If he's big enough to try to comfort me, he's big enough to start learning the tools of the trade. I only let him fire the .22, but he is a deadeye marksman. My drill sergeant would have taken him over me in a second. Times like this, I sure am proud of my boy. I have a feeling it'll be different with Sammy. Maybe he's just too young to show it, but I don't think he's got the same kind of killer instinct.

Pliny the Younger, letter to Sura:

There was at Athens a large and roomy house, which had a bad name, so that no one could live there. In the dead of the night a noise, resembling the clashing of iron, was frequently heard, which, if you listened more attentively, sounded like the rattling of chains, distant at first, but approaching nearer by degrees: immediately afterward a spectre appeared in the form of an old man, of extremely emaciated and squalid appearance, with a long beard and dishevelled hair, rattling the chains on his feet and hands. The distressed occupants meanwhile passed their wakeful nights under the most dreadful terrors imaginable. This, as it broke their rest, ruined their health, and brought on distempers, their terror grew upon them, and death ensued. Even in the daytime, though the spirit did not appear, yet the impression remained so strong upon their imaginations that it still seemed before their eyes, and kept them in perpetual alarm. Consequently the house was at length deserted, as being deemed absolutely uninhabitable; so that it was now entirely abandoned to the ghost. However, in hopes that some tenant might be found who was ignorant of this very alarming circumstance, a bill was put up, giving notice that it was either to be let or sold. It happened that Athenodorus the philosopher came to Athens at this time, and, reading the bill, enquired the price. The extraordinary cheapness raised his suspicion; nevertheless, when he heard the whole story, he was so far from being discouraged that he was more strongly inclined to hire it, and, in short, actually did so. When it grew toward evening, he ordered a couch to be prepared for him in the front part of the house, and, after calling for a light, together with his pencil and tablets, directed all his people to retire. But that his mind might not, for want of employment, be open to the vain terrors of imaginary noises and spirits, he applied himself to writing with the utmost attention. The first part of the night passed in entire silence, as usual; at length a clanking of iron and rattling of chains was heard: however, he neither lifted up his eyes nor laid down his pen, but in order to keep calm and collected, tried to pass the sounds off to himself as something else. The noise increased and advanced nearer, till it seemed at the door, and at last in the chamber. He looked up, saw, and recognized the ghost exactly as it had been described to him: it stood before him, beckoning with a finger, like a person who calls another. Athenodorus in reply made a sign with his hand that it should wait a little, and threw his eyes again upon his papers; the ghost then rattled its chains over the head of the philosopher, who looked upon this, and seeing it beckoning as before, immediately arose, and, light in hand, followed it. The ghost slowly stalked along, as if encumbered with its chains, and, turning into the area of the house, suddenly vanished. Atheno-dorus, being thus deserted, made a mark with some grass and leaves on the spot where the spirit left him. The next day he gave information to the magistrates, and advised them to order that spot to be dug up. This was accordingly done, and the skeleton of a man in chains was found there; for the body, having lain a considerable time in the ground, was putrefied and moldered away from the fetters. The bones being collected together were publicly buried, and thus after the ghost was appeased by the proper ceremonies, the house was haunted no more.

1986

January 1:

Happy New Year. This year, Mary, I will find out what killed you.

January 24:

For his seventh birthday, I took Dean shooting again. He wanted to fire one of the big guns—that's what he called them. I let him shoot the Browning, but I steadied his hands. Sammy wanted me to help him make Dean a card. It was like a normal day, like we were a normal family with a mom who was off shopping or at work or something. Instead of dead. That illusion never lasts. I can't afford to let it.

> The wicked Utukku who slays man alive on the plain.
> The wicked Alû who covers (man) like a garment.
> The wicked Etimmu, the wicked Gallû, who
>   bind the body.
> The Lamme (Lamashtu), the Lammea (Labasu),
>   who cause disease in the body.
> The Lilû who wanders in the plain.
> They have come nigh unto a suffering man
>   on the outside.
> They have brought about a painful malady
>   in his body.

The curse of evil has come into his body.
An evil goblin they have placed in his body.
An evil bane has come into his body.
Evil poison they have placed in his body.
An evil malediction has come into his parts.
Evil and trouble they have placed in his body.
Poison and taint have come into his body.
They have produced evil.
Evil being, evil face, evil mouth, evil tongue.
Sorcery, venom, slaver, wicked machinations,
Which are produced in the body of the sick man.
O woe for the sick man whom they cause to
*   moan like a ṣaharrat-pot.*

January 29:

RIP
Jarvis
Resnik
Smith
Onizuka
McAuliffe
McNair
Scobee

April 16:

There's a reason why they call it Devil's Gate.

We were supposed to turn Devil's Gate into a devil's trap. But I made a mistake, and Bill died.

It's a slot canyon, used to flood all the time (Arroyo Seco isn't always *seco*) until they put in a spillway and built the reservoir. But odd things happened there. Four kids in three years, from 1957–1960, vanish without a trace. Other people see things. No one will talk about it. Bill was sure that something had come up through the canyon thirty years ago, and was about to again. Some kind of hellspawn. So we went there to catch it in the act and take care of it. Hellspawn, that's the word he used. I don't know if I believe in Hell. But I do remember the Black Shuck, and the way Mary's spirit was transformed in Blue Earth. That came from somewhere. Was it a demon? I don't know if I believe in demons. I've seen people who thought they were demons, and acted like demons—but how would you know the difference between a demon and a shape-shifter? How would you know?

I'm avoiding it. This is how Bill died.

At the mouth of the spillway we found this godawful fluid trickling straight out of the concrete. Dark brown, stinking of sulfur. It burned your fingers to touch it. Bill drew a figure around it, he called it a Devil's Trap from a book called the Key of Solomon. Psalm 90:13. He used charcoal to draw the trap on the wall of the spillway around the sulfur, and then I laid it out on the ground in front of the tunnel, using salt. Kosher salt, no added iodides. Bill said this was important. He started watching the sky as the sun set. The first stars would tell him when the hellspawn was coming through, he said. I looked up with him, but the stars just looked like stars to me. I have so much to learn. There I was in Pasadena, the boys back at the roadhouse. I wasn't being a father. I was being a hunter. I was hunting. And while I looked up at the sky, I made a simple mistake. I didn't pay attention to where my feet were, and I scuffed the salt. Just a little. But enough that when something came out of the mouth of the tunnel, nothing stopped it.

It looked like smoke, and sounded like a million flies. Bill looked down from the stars just in time for it to flow right into him. He started jerking like a condemned man in the electric chair, and two voices were coming out of his mouth. One was the thing, the hellspawn. I don't know what language it was speaking, but its voice was horrible. It was the sound cancer would make if it could talk. And Bill, he kept saying over and over again, John, shoot me, shoot me, John.

So I did.

It was the worst mistake I ever made. It was careless and stupid and it got a good man killed. A husband and father, and a damned good hunter, and I don't know how I'm going to explain this to Ellen. And Jo, poor Jo. She's four years old. How am I going to tell her? I can't just let Ellen do it. I'm responsible. It was over in less than a minute, Bill Harvelle dead and me standing there with a gun in my hand listening to the echo of the gunshots in the hills and the echo of that awful hellspawn voice in my head.

And to the end, Bill was teaching me. With his body dying and something inside him, he staggered over to the sulfur-stinking wall and let the smoke back out—straight into the Devil's Trap on the wall. Then he took a step back, careful not to do what I did, and then he sat down and died leaning against the spillway wall under the Devil's Trap he'd drawn. He saved my life even though I took his. It was a hunter's death.

I copied the Devil's Trap, but I didn't need to. I couldn't forget it if I wanted to.

May 2:

Tahlequah, OK. Sammy is three years old today. We celebrated with an ice-cream cake. He was still wearing most of it when he fell asleep. Dean's sleeping too, the two of them in the bed. The room only has one bed. I'll sleep on the floor, if I sleep at all. Some nights it's enough to watch them sleep, and know that if they start to have a nightmare I'll be right there to stop it.

May 17:

This would have been our eighth anniversary. Eight is bronze.

September 5:

Dean started second grade. I watch him like a hawk. He makes me swear that I'll take good care of Sammy before he'll go to school. God, I love that kid. I have the days with Sammy while Dean is learning whatever kids learn in second grade. Sammy's a very different kid. He hasn't taken to the idea of hunting bad guys, and he's still too young to really under-stand what it means to avenge his mother. To him, her death just means she's not here, and he doesn't remember her. For him, Mary is a word. A mother, to him, is something he never had—but he's still supposed to be sad that she died. I don't think he gets it. How could he, really?

October 30:

I saw an exorcism today. Or something that looked like an exorcism. According to Jim, there really are demons. I don't know if I believe that—he's a pastor, so of course he does, but . . . demons? From Hell? Even after the things I've seen these past three years (almost), I can't quite make demons fit. But between watching what happened to Bill at Devil's Gate, and what I saw today . . . I don't know.

Jim knows I have the journal. After he was done, and the girl was looking around like someone who'd just woken up from the worst nightmare you can imagine, he took me back to his church and had me copy down a shorter version of the Rituale Romanum exorcism ritual. Usually, he said, you don't have to read the whole thing. Most demons can't hold out that long. But he wants me to copy the whole thing just in case. So I'm going to. I don't know if I believe in demons, but I'm not sure I can disbelieve them anymore, either.

> *In the expulsion of demonic forces or energie residing in an individual, soul possession, command of one's motor and abilities.*

The Rituale Romanum was widely used in the mid- to late 13th century in most of eastern Europe until the church banned its use in the beginning of the 14th century. Initial studies indicate that this anti-curse was particularly helpful in ridding the individual of unwanted guests. The first part of the ritual expels the entity from the host. The second half of the ritual banishes the spirit back from whence it came. Repeat the incantation as follows:

> 1. *Regna Terrae, cantate deo,*
> *psallite domino,*
> *qui vehitur per calus*
> *caelos antiquos!*
>
> *Ecce, edit vocem suam, vocem potentem:*
> *Akinoscite potentiam dei!*

Majestas ejus,
Et potentia ejus
In nubibus.

2. *Timendus est dues e sancto suo,*
   dues Israel; ipse potentiam
   datet robur populo suo
   benedictus dues.

   Gloria Patri.

On the completion of the first part of the incantation the demon may take one or more of several forms ranging from liquid to gaseous to corporeal to any combination of the afore-mentioned. Great care must be taken in performing the second part of the ritual. The demon upon expulsion can become very powerful without the need of a host. Beware that the spirit can enter a host through any opening in the host. Keep your eyes open and mouth shut.

In Michigan, they call October 30 Devil's Night.

November 2:

Mary has been dead for three years. She doesn't know that Sammy has learned the alphabet, and likes to catch bugs. She doesn't know that Dean watches his little brother like a hawk every minute, with an expression on his face that says he's willing to die to keep Sammy safe. She doesn't know how it tears me up inside to see that expression, and to know that it's there because I have drilled it into Dean that Sammy is his responsibility. He's eight years old, and I've told him his brother's life is in his hands. Mary, I didn't have any right to do that. But what else could I do?

1987

January 1:

Another New Year. Another promise. I will find it, Mary. And kill it.

Tracked down the complete Rituale Romanum, the version the exorcists like to use when they have plenty of time. Hope I'll never need it.

OREMUS ORATIO

Deus, et pater Domini nostri Jesu Christi, invoco nomen sanctum tuum, et clementiam tuam supplex exposco: ut adversus hunc, et omnem immundum spiritum, qui vexat hoc plasma tuum. Mihi auxilium praestare igneris. Per eumdem Dominum. Amen.

EXORCISMUS

Exorcizo te, immundissime spiritus, omnis incursio adversarii, omne phantasma, omnis legio, in nomine Domini nostri Jesu Christi eradicare, et effugare ab hoc plasmate Dei. Ipse tibi imperat, qui te de supernis caelorum in inferiora terrae demergi praecepit. Ipse tibi imperat, qui mari, ventis, et tempestatibus impersvit. Audi ergo, et time, satana, inimice fidei, hostis generis humani, mortis adductor, vitae raptor, justitiae declinator, malorum radix, fomes vitiorum, seductor hominum, proditor gentium, incitator invidiae, origo avaritiae, causa discordiae, excitator dolorum: quid stas, et resistis, cum scias. Christum Dominum vias tuas perdere? Illum metue, qui in Isaac immolatus est, in Joseph venumdatus, in sgno occisus, in homine crucifixus, deinde inferni triumphator fuit. Sequentes cruces fiant in fronte obsessi. Recede ergo in nomine Patris et Filii, et Spiritus Sancti: da locum Spiritui Sancto, per hoc signum sanctae Cruci Jesu Christi Domini nostri: Qui cum Patre et eodem Spiritu Sancto vivit et regnat Deus. Per omnia saecula saeculorum. Amen.

OREMUS ORATIO

Deus, conditor et defensor generis humani, qui hominem ad imaginem tuam formasti; respice super hunc famulum tuum (N)., qui dolis immundi spiritus appetitur, quem vetus adversarius, antiquus hostis terrae, formidinis horrore circumvolat, et sensum mentis humanae stupore defigit, terrore contrubat, et metu trepidi timoris exagitat. Repelle, Domine, virtutem diaboli, fallacesque ejus insidias amove: procul impius tentator aufugiat: sit nominis tui signo (in fronte) famulus tuus munitus et in animo tutus et corpore (tres cruces sequentes fiant in pectore daemoniaci). Tu pectoris hujus interna custodias. Tu viscera regas. Tu cor confirmes. In anima adversatricis potestatis tentamenta evanescant. Da, Domine, ad hanc invocationem sanctissimi nominis tui gratiam, ut, qui hucusque terrebat, territus aufugiat, et victus abscedat, tibique possit hic famulus tuus et corde firmatus et mente sincerus, debitum praebere famulatum. Per Dominum. Amen.

EXORCISMUS

Adjuro te, serpens antique, per judicem vivorum et mortuorum, per factorem tuum, per factorem mundi, per eum, qui habet potestatem mittendi te in gehennam, ut ab hoc famulo Dei (N)., ad Ecclesiae sinum recurrit, cum metu, et exercitu furoris tui festinus discedas. Adjuro te iterum (in fronte) non mea infirmitate, sed virtute Spiritus Sancti, ut exeas ab hoc famulo Dei (N)., quem omnipotens Deus ad imaginem suam fecit. Cede igitur, cede non mihi, sed ministro Christi. Illius enim te urget potestas, qui te Cruci suae subjugavit. Illius brachium contremisce, qui devictis gemitibus inferni, animas ad lucem perduxit. Sit tibi terror corpus hominis (in pectore), sit tibi formido imago Dei (in fronte). Non resistas, nec moreris discedere ab homine isto, quoniam complacuit Christo in homine habitare. Et ne contemnendum putes, dum me peccatorem nimis esse cognoscis. Imperat tibi Deus. Imperat tibi majestas Christi Imperat tibi Deus Pater, imoerat tibi Deus Filius, imperat tibi Deus Spiritus Sanctus. Imperat tibi sacramentum Crucis. Imperat tibi fides sanctorum Apostolorum Petri et Pauli, et ceterorum Sanctorum. Imperat tibi Martyrum sanguis, Imperat tibi contentia Confessorum. Imperat tibi pia Sanctorum et Sanctarum omnium intercessio, Imperat tibi christianae fidei mysteriorum virtus. Exi ergo, transgressor. Exi, seducor, plene omni dolo et fallacia, virtutis inimice, innocentium persecutor. Da locum, dirissime, da loocum, impiissime, da locum Christo, in quo nihil invevisti de operibus tuis: qui te spoliavit, qui regnum tuum destruxit, qui te victum ligavit, et vasa tua diripuit: qui te projecit in tenebras exteriores, ubi tibi cum ministris tuis erit praeparatus

interitus. Sed quid truculente reniteris? Quid temera-
rie detrectas? Reus es omnipotenti Deo, cujus stat-
uta transgressus es. Reus es Filio ejus Jesu Christo
Domino nostro, quem tentare ausus es, et crucifigere
praesumpsisti. Reus es humano generi, cui tuis per-
suasionibus mortis venenum propinasti. Adjuro ergo
te, draco nequissime, in nomine Agni immaculati, qui
ambulavit super aspidem et basiliscum, qui conculavit
leonem et draconem, ut discedas ab hoc homine (fiat
signum crucis in fronte), discedas ab Ecclesia Dei
(fiat signum crucis super circumstantes): contremisce,
et effuge, invocato nomine Domini illius, quem inferi
tremunt: cui Virtutes caelorum, et Potestates, et Dom-
inationes subjectae sunt: quem Cherubim et Seraphim
indefessis vocibus laudant, dicentes: Sanctus, sanctus,
sanctus Dominus Deus Sabaoth. Imperat tibi Verbum
caro factum. Imperat tibi natus ex Virgine. Imperat
tibi Jesus Nazarenus, qui te, cum disciplulos ejus con-
temneres, elisum atque prostratum exire praecepit ab
homine: quo praesente, cum te ab homine serparasset,
nec porcorum gregem ingredi praesumebas. Recede
ergo nunc adjuratus in nomine ejus ab homine, quem
ipse plasmavit. Durum est tibi velle resistere. Durum
est tibi contra stimulum calcitrare, Quia quanto tar-
dius exis, tanto magis tibi supplicium crescit, quia non
homines contemnis, sed illum, qui dominatur vivorum
et mortuorum, qui venturus est judicare vivos et mor-
tuos, et saeculum per ignem. Amen.

OREMUS ORATIO
Deus caeli, Deus terrae, Deus Angelorum, Deus
Archangelorum, Deus Prophetarum, Deus Apos-
tolorum, Deus Martyrum, Deus Virginum, Deus,

qui potestatem habes donare vitam post mortem, requiem post laborem: quia non est alius Deus praeter te, nec esse poterit verus, nisi tu, Creator caeli et terrae, qui verus Rex es, et cujus regni non erit finis; humiliter majestati gloriae tuae supplico, ut hunc famulum tuum de immundis spiritibus liberare digneris. Per Christum Dominum Nostrum. Amen.

EXORCISMUS

Adjuro ergo te, omnis immundissime spiritus, omne phantasma, omnis incursio satanae, in nomine Jesu Christi Nazareni, qui post lavacrum Joannis in desrtum ductus est, et te in tuis sedibus vicit: ut, quem ille de limo terrae ad honorem gloriae suae formavit, tu desinas impurgnare: et in homine miserabili non humanam fragilitatem, sed imaginem omnipotentis Dei contremiscas. Cede ergo Deo qui te, et malitiam tuam in Pharaone, et in exercitu ejus per Moysen servum suum in abysseum demersit. Cede Deo qui te per fidelissimum servum suum David de rege Saule spiritualibus canticis pulsum fugavit. Cede Deo qui te in Juda Iscariote proditore damnavit. Ille enim te divinis verberibus tangit, in cujus conspectu cum tuis legionibus tremens et clamans dixisti; quid nobis et tibi, Jesu, Fili Dei altissimi? Venisti huc ante tempus torquere nos? Ille te perpetuis flammis urget, qui in fine temporum dicturus est impiis: Discedite a me, maledicti, in ignem aeternum, qui paratus est diabolo et angelis ejus. Tibi enim, impie, et angelis tuis vermes erunt, qui numquam morientur. Tibi, et angelis tuis inexstinguibile praeparatur incendium: quia tu es princeps maledicti homicidii, tu auctor incestus, tu sacrilegorum caput, tu actionum pessimarum mag-

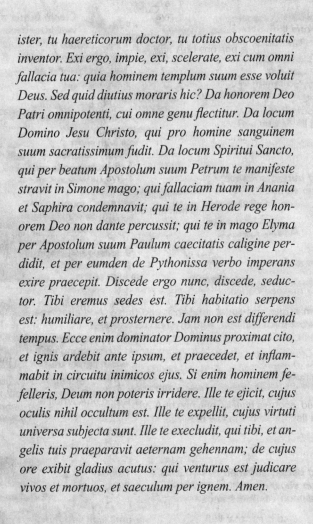

ister, tu haereticorum doctor, tu totius obscoenitatis inventor. Exi ergo, impie, exi, scelerate, exi cum omni fallacia tua: quia hominem templum suum esse voluit Deus. Sed quid diutius moraris hic? Da honorem Deo Patri omnipotenti, cui omne genu flectitur. Da locum Domino Jesu Christo, qui pro homine sanguinem suum sacratissimum fudit. Da locum Spiritui Sancto, qui per beatum Apostolum suum Petrum te manifeste stravit in Simone mago; qui fallaciam tuam in Anania et Saphira condemnavit; qui te in Herode rege honorem Deo non dante percussit; qui te in mago Elyma per Apostolum suum Paulum caecitatis caligine perdidit, et per eumden de Pythonissa verbo imperans exire praecepit. Discede ergo nunc, discede, seductor. Tibi eremus sedes est. Tibi habitatio serpens est: humiliare, et prosternere. Jam non est differendi tempus. Ecce enim dominator Dominus proximat cito, et ignis ardebit ante ipsum, et praecedet, et inflammabit in circuitu inimicos ejus. Si enim hominem fefelleris, Deum non poteris irridere. Ille te ejicit, cujus oculis nihil occultum est. Ille te expellit, cujus virtuti universa subjecta sunt. Ille te execludit, qui tibi, et angelis tuis praeparavit aeternam gehennam; de cujus ore exibit gladius acutus: qui venturus est judicare vivos et mortuos, et saeculum per ignem. Amen.

January 24:

Dean turns eight today. Second grade is treating him well. I hope we can stay. He's at school, and they're going to have a little party for him. Then when he gets home, we're going to do the family thing. We're going to Chuck E. Cheese's, and we'll eat pizza and play video games until the kids go nuts.

May 2:

Sammy is four today. And sure enough, we're in Colorado. That's three out of four birthdays we've been visiting Daniel. The mountains are a good place to spend early May. Maybe we should make a tradition of it—but I have a feeling that we're not in any place to start traditions. I had to pull Dean out of school when I got a note from Ellen that someone passing through the roadhouse had just exorcised a demon that knew where we were.

I think hunters call something a demon when they don't know what it is. The word is easy to throw around. But whatever it was, if the Winchesters were on its mind, it's the enemy. So we're moving for two reasons. One, the enemy knows where we are. Two, I'm going to go after him where he is . . . as soon as I figure that out. So we're in Colorado, on our way to Texas. Dean understands.

Sammy gets Daniel's books down from the shelves and pretends to read them. He can pick out some words, but what he's really after is the pictures. Like any kid his age. We stopped by here because I took out a strange kind of revenant in April, one I've never seen before. It was in Greektown, Detroit. Daniel figured it out right away.

VRYKOLAKAS: Unconsecrated burial, returns to either murder people in the graveyard or cause problems in the house it left. Sometimes appears as human, other times as a sort of werewolf (although in some versions, the vrykolakas is destroyed by being dug up and eaten by a wolf). Can drain the life force of the sleeper, similar to succubus/incubus or mara.

Stories vary widely, often incorporating elements of the poltergeist. Sometimes the vrykolakas attacks and kills people; other times it plagues their sleep; other times only children die; other times it is only waiting to be dispatched by its surviving family members' fulfillment of a promise. Much overlap between vrykolakas lore and that of vampires. Not sure if one is a subspecies of the other, or if confusion in the lore has obscured the real differences.

VETALA: Hostile spirits from Indian lore, will animate corpses—their own or others—to move around. Haunt cemeteries and creation grounds. Will attack in cemeteries; can also drive people mad. Will kill children, possibly to eat, and are known to induce miscarriages. Trapped between the material world and the afterlife, can be dispelled by the performance of funeral rites. NOTE: Exorcism will not work on a vetala. They aren't demons in the sense of the Judeo-Christian ritual. If caught in the right mood, a vetala might tell you the past and future; for this reason they're much sought after by sorcerers . . . mostly resulting in fatal mishaps for those sorcerers, since if caught in the wrong mood, a vetala is lethal before you know it's there. Best idea is to get on with the funeral rites and send them on their way.

May 17:

This would have been our ninth anniversary. Pottery. How is six years iron and nine pottery? I wonder if we would have had more children. Mary talked about a girl sometimes. I would have liked having a daughter.

It's summer, we're on the move. Already I'm trying to figure out what to do about school in the fall. I'm starting to figure out that you can move a kid from school to school every month, and the schools deal with it because they have to. A part of me wonders how the kid deals with it.

But sons have to be soldiers. And soldiers adapt.

July 13:

From the mouths of babes . . . we were in Portland, Maine, because I'd heard of a Miqmaq shaman named David Fowler who lived there. I told him some of my story, and he agreed to raise a manitou and let me ask it some questions. We went down into the basement of his house and he started getting the divination ready. I'm the only white man who's ever seen it, he said, and he was only doing it for me as a favor to the other hunters he knew. He burned sacred tobacco, and some other herbs I didn't recognize. The room got more smoky than it seems like it should have. The manitou appeared, and I got right to the point. I asked it who or what killed Mary. And then things went wrong.

I still don't know whether Fowler made a mistake, or whether a different spirit rode up into our world along with the manitou. But whatever happened, it turned into something physical and real. Like a bear, kind of. And before I could stop it, it killed Fowler. It almost killed me too, but I fought it. I don't know if I would have won, because the spirit let go of its form, animated Fowler's body, and went out through the basement window. I got the hell out of there and picked up the boys. We were almost to the New Hampshire state line and I'd told Dean a little about what had happened, because I was so frustrated and ashamed that I had to talk to someone. Sammy was asleep the whole time.

Then Dean asked me one of those killer questions that

little kids come up with. "Dad," he says. "Won't the manitou go after other people now?"

That's a hard thing to face. Not that he asked the question, or that he was right, but that he had a better sense of right and wrong than I did. We were back at Fowler's house an hour later, and that night I tracked him down and killed him. He was prowling around the edges of a Cub Scout campout in a place called Bradbury Mountain. God knows what would have happened if Dean hadn't spoken up.

I came this close to going completely off the rails. I almost let this quest overwhelm what I know is right, and a bunch of kids almost died because of it. A hunter never passes up a hunt, and a hunter never bails out on a hunt. That will never happen again. Never. I will not fail Mary's memory, and I will not fail the boys.

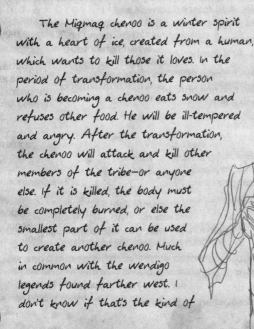

The Miqmaq chenoo is a winter spirit with a heart of ice, created from a human, which wants to kill those it loves. In the period of transformation, the person who is becoming a chenoo eats snow and refuses other food. He will be ill-tempered and angry. After the transformation, the chenoo will attack and kill other members of the tribe—or anyone else. If it is killed, the body must be completely burned, or else the smallest part of it can be used to create another chenoo. Much in common with the wendigo legends found farther west. I don't know if that's the kind of

45

spirit that caught Fowler. It was summer; I don't think so. But when I went back to his house, I took a book. I read a dead man's book. Next time I'll be ready.

November 2:

Mary has been dead for four years. Dean asked me today what she looked like. He never talks about her on any other day but this one. I couldn't even show him a picture, so I told him what you tell a boy who asks about his dead mother. I told him that she was beautiful and kind and she loved him and Sammy more than anything in the world.

1988

January 24:

Dean turns nine today. We're on the move, so he might not finish third grade. He calls himself the New Kid all the time. He's been in three schools already this year. Who knows how many more?

April 14:

SALT

Symbol of permanence, incorruptibility. The word "salvation" originates from the use of salt in sealing covenants. Jews in the Temple offered salt, still use it in Sabbath rituals. Leviticus 2:13: "And every oblation of thy meat offering shalt thou season with salt; neither shalt thou suffer the salt of the covenant of thy God to be lacking from thy meat offering: with all thine offerings thou shalt offer salt." Lot's wife turns to salt as a reminder of permanence of errors. In II Kings, Elisha purifies a spring with salt. Jesus coined the phrase "salt of the earth" for apostles, because of their commitment. Salt used in some Catholic consecration rituals. Spilled salt should never be picked up; the bad luck is balanced by throwing salt over the shoulder at the demons who approach because of the spill. Buddhist tradition holds that salt repels all evil spirits. Throw salt over your shoulder before entering your house after attending a funeral; will prevent spirits clinging from the funeral from getting in. Salt used to purify in Shinto and other traditions; Shinto myth says first landmass, Onogoro Shima, arose when salt separated from a world ocean. Native American tribes in the Southwest restricted who could eat salt. Hopi legends about the preciousness of salt held that location of salt deposits—hard to get to, dangerous to work—was a punishment from the Warrior Twins.

Practical uses: a line of salt is a barrier no spirit can cross. Mediums use lines to constrain movements of summoned spirits. In Japanese folklore, ghosts are packed in jars full of salt. A double-barrel load of rock salt will dispel the ectoplasmic manifestation of a spirit. When destroying a spirit permanently, salt the remains or focus of the haunting before burning. "The devil loveth no salt in his meat." Scottish fishermen used to throw salt into the ocean to blind malicious faeries.

In Norse myth, ancestor of the gods was born from a salt lick.

Dark side of salt: salt the earth after a battle so that nothing will grow, no one will live there. Can be reversed to a symbol of barrenness.

Myth among Caribbean slaves that Africans—Igbo, in particular—can fly because they did not eat salt in their native country.

MUST BE ROCK SALT—IODIZED SALT IMPURE, WILL NOT WORK.

May 2:

Sammy is five today. Thank God. He almost didn't make it.

I could blame Dean, but it's my fault. There's enough blame to go around. I missed the kill, and I left Dean watching Sam, and he couldn't pull the trigger when he needed to. I haven't taught him well enough. If he is weak like that again, my boys will die . . . but what kind of father am I to put a nine-year-old boy in a situation where he might have to kill to protect his brother?

I'm the kind of father I have to be. I'm the kind of father who teaches his boys that no man or monster can kill their mother and get away with it. I'm the kind of father who shows them that when it comes to family, you go to the ends of the earth to put things right.

We're in Wisconsin, so we might as well skip over to Blue Earth and check in with Jim. He'll want to know about this, and maybe it'll do me good to talk to him.

Reminder: Tell Jim about the Hausa, an African tribe whose witches keep magical stones in their stomachs. They eat their victims' souls slowly, causing the victim to waste away and die. Also, they can turn into dogs. Another African witch, sukuyadyo or obayifo, bind victims magically and drain their blood or life force. Sukuyadyo can change their skins, hiding their real skin under a pot or mortar in their house and taking on the appearance of another. Related to skinwalker, also variations on medieval European vampire legends. Obayifo transformed into a ball of light to drain life force. (Will-o'-the-wisp.)

Time for Sammy to learn how to read.

Jiangshi: "Hopping corpse." Reanimated corpses out of Chinese lore that kill living

49

creatures to feed on _spiritus vitae_ (qi). Possible that they are restricted to roadways, but I'm working from a story Bobby Singer told me here. Never seen one.

May 17:

This would have been our tenth anniversary. Tin.

September 28:

Séance:

On a clean altar cloth, place a small bowl filled with fresh herbs. Around the perimeter of the cloth, place black and white candles, alternating and equal in number. When all of the candles are lit, recite the following:

> _Amate spiritus obscure, te quaerimus._
> _Te oramus, nobiscum colloquere, apud nos circita._

At the finish of the incantation, pinch a tiny amount of frankincense, sandalwood, or cinnamon powder over one of the candle flames.

Pythagoras also led séances in approximately 540 B.C., using something like a Ouija board. Using a wheeled table that moved toward signs set up in a rough circle, Pythagoras and his student Philolaus interpreted the motions as spirit signals.

Here Perimedes and Eurylochus held the victims, while I drew my sword and dug the trench a cubit each way. I made a drink-offering to all the dead, first with honey and milk, then with wine, and thirdly with water, and I sprinkled white barley meal over the whole, praying earnestly to the poor feckless ghosts, *and promising them that when I got back to Ithaca I would sacrifice a barren heifer for them, the best I had, and would load the pyre with good things. I also particularly promised that Teiresias should have a black sheep to himself, the best in all my flocks. When I had prayed sufficiently to the dead, I cut the throats of the two sheep and let the blood run into the trench, whereon the ghosts came trooping up from Erebus—brides, young bachelors, old men worn out with toil, maids who had been crossed in love, and brave men who had been killed in battle, with their armour still smirched with blood; they came from every quarter and flitted round the trench with a strange kind of screaming sound that made me turn pale with fear. When I saw them coming I told the men to be quick and flay the carcasses of the two dead sheep and make burnt offerings of them, and at the same time to repeat prayers to Hades and to Proserpine; but I sat where I was with my sword drawn and would not let the poor feckless ghosts come near the blood till Teiresias should have answered my questions.*

Katabasis: the voyage to the underworld—Orpheus looking for Eurydice. Adapted to Greek necromancy. A spirit projection of the necromancer would travel to the underworld to speak with the dead.

Katadesmoi: A Greek curse inscribed on a lead tablet (usually). A spirit is summoned and bound to the tablet to make sure the curse is effective. Term also used for the summoning and binding of a spirit to a task. Katadesmoi buried in a cemetery or sacred place to make them more effective.

51

. . . souls after death do as yet love their body which they left, as those souls do whose bodies want due burial or have left their bodies by violent death, and as yet wander about their carcasses in a troubled and moist spirit, being, as it were, allured by something that hath an affinity with them . . .

Necromantic conjuration from Reginald Scot, Discoverie of Witchcraft. Seals of the Earth necessary to bring the spirit.

FIRST fast and praie three daies, and absteine thee from all filthinesse; go to one that is new buried, such a one as killed himselfe or destroied himselfe wilfullie: or else get thee promise of one that shalbe hanged, and let him sweare an oth to thee, after his bodie is dead, that his spirit shall come to thee, and doo thee true service, at thy commandements, in all dales, houres, and minuts. And let no persons see thy doings, but thy fellow. And about eleven a clocke in the night, go to the place where he was buried, and saie with a bold faith & hartie desire, to have the spirit come that thou doost call for, thy fellow having a candle in his left hand, and in his right hand a christall stone, and saie these words following, the maister having a hazell wand in his right hand, and these names of God written thereupon, Tetragrammaton + Adonay + Agla + Craton + Then strike three strokes on the ground, and saie;

Arise N. Arise N. Arise N. I conjure thee spirit N. by the resurrection of our Lord Jesu Christ, that thou doo obey to my words, and come unto me this night verelie and trulie, as thou beleevest to be saved at the daie of judgement. And I will sweare to thee on oth, by the perill of my soule, that if thou wilt come to me, and appeare to me this night, and shew me true visions in this christall stone, and fetch me the fairie Sibylia, that I may talke with hir visiblie, and she may come before me, as the conjuration leadeth: and in so doing, I will give thee an almesse deed, and praie for thee N. to my Lord God, wherby thou maiest be restored to thy salvation at the resurrection daie, to be received as one of the elect of God, to the everlasting glorie, Amen.

Sibly, necromantic conjuration. At the tomb or grave, after inscribing the protective circle: "By the virtue of the holy resurrection, and the torments of the damned, I conjure and exorcise thee, spirit of N. deceased, to answer my liege demands, being obedient unto these sacred ceremonies, on pain of everlasting torment and distress. Arise, arise, arise, I charge and command thee."

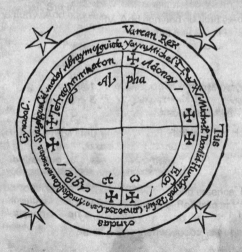

November 2:

Mary has been dead for five years. We were married for five years. I feel like I'm serving a sentence sometimes, and the only way to get out of this prison is to find whoever or whatever took her away from me.

December 5:

Dean's teacher called to tell me that he got a subscription to the *Weekly World News*, and had it delivered to school. How is he paying for it? I could ask him, but he's already too sharp to give me a straight answer. And I could force him to, but there's no point. If that makes him feel more at home in his world . . .

December 27:

A variation, supposed to be for summoning and speaking to angels. But I've never met a hunter who believed in angels. Not even the ones who have seen demons.

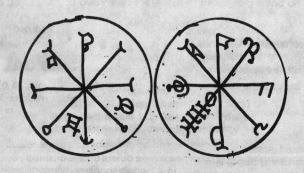

1989

January 24:

Dean turns ten today. Reagan out of office. A crazy hunter told me a couple of years ago that Reagan was an avatar of the Antichrist because each of his names has six letters: Ronald Wilson Reagan. Reagan also lived at 666 St. Cloud Road.

Possible that original number of the Beast was 616. This is attested to in Codex Ephraimi Rescriptus. St. Jerome said 616 instead of 666. 666 a triangular number (1+2+3+4+5 . . . +36), better symmetry than 616.

616: area code of western Michigan—Kalamazoo, Grand Rapids, Traverse City.

Fear of the number 666: hexakosioihexekontahexaphobia.

Gematria: Hebrew numerology, values later transposed to other alphabets. According to gematria, commentators on Revelations give possible names of the Antichrist:

Lampetis = the lustrous one
Teitan = ?
Palaibaskanos = ancient sorcerer
Benediktos = blue bastard
Kakos Odegos = wicked guide
Alethes Blaberos = harmful
Amnos Adikos = unjust lamb

O Niketes = the conqueror
Antemos = opponent
Diclux = double-dealer (same as Teitan, only Latin)
Genserikos = Genseric, Vandal who sacked Rome?
Arnodymy = I deny
Acxyme = ?

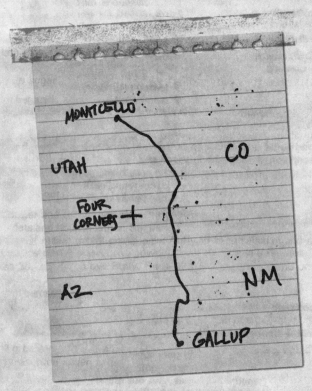

Hound sightings?

May 2:

Sammy is six years old today. He'll start kindergarten in the fall. Wherever we are. He's such a different kid than Dean. Quiet, watchful. He's learned that there are things to fear in the world, but where Dean wants to fight them, you get the sense that Sammy watches, learns. He's figuring something out. But when Sammy does ask a question, it's a good one.

May 13:

May 17:

This would have been our eleventh anniversary. Steel.

June 10:

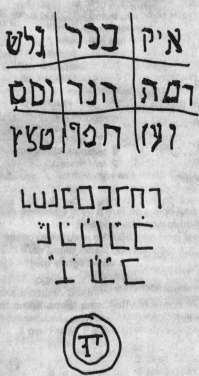

July 4:

This is how you spend your holiday weekends when you're a hunter.

I got Sammy and Dean into a day camp not too far from Blue Earth, so I could consult with Pastor Jim about a few things while the boys got to be regular kids for a while. Should have known that not even summer camp could be normal for the Winchesters. On the fifth day of the camp, Dean was canoeing through an easy rapids on the Blue Earth River. Things went bad. Dean swore to me when he came back that he'd seen something—only he said "someone"—capsize the canoe. I didn't think about it too much . . . until the next week, when another canoe went over and the counselor paddling it died. I spent a couple of days looking into it, and ran across a Cree legend about humanoid tricksters called mannegishi. They live in river rapids and like to tip canoes, but they usually don't get malevolent unless the locals do something to make them angry. So what was it?

Turns out the camp is expanding, and part of the work involved blasting some riverside rock formations that used to have pictographs showing the Cree's reverence for the little bastards. The mannegishi didn't like having those gone, and started to take it out on the campers.

I'd have killed every one of them for coming after Dean, but the truth is they had a right to be mad. So I kept my head and got Jim to put me in touch with a Cree medicine man who lived over in South Dakota. I complained about the distance, and Jim told me to shut up and be happy I didn't have to go to Montana or Saskatchewan, where most of the Cree live now. The medicine man called himself Joey Tall Pine, which I figure is a moniker he took on for the tourists, but after the last six years, I'm the last guy in the world who gets to complain about someone using an alias. I gave him a ride back to Blue Earth and we went down to the rapids that night (now two days ago). He talked things over with the mannegishi, and they struck a bargain. They'd stop going after kids at the camp if Joey redid some of the pictographs somewhere and guaranteed that they wouldn't be destroyed. Jim stepped in and said, hey, I don't have nearly enough aquatic tricksters in the creek behind my house. Presto—mannegishi in Jim's creek, and Joey Tall Pine got to exercise his pictographic talent.

Part of me still wants to kill them, because of what happened to Dean, but when I take a minute to cool off I realize that it's the camp's fault. Some day camp, wrecking pictographs so they can expand their boat launch. The boys are going someplace else next week, for as long as we can stay.

Anyway, it's over now. Fireworks going off, I've got a couple of beers in me, the boys are asleep in a tent out in Jim's backyard. For the moment, the battle pauses. Mary, I can't fight every minute.

August 18:

Other water spirits I've read up on:

Vodyanoy. Russian male water spirit, sometimes said to be a shape-shifter but more often appears as an old man, skin freckled with scales, a green beard tangled with muck and underwater plants. May live in whirlpools. In larger bodies of water, often lives in sunken ships, served by the drowned ghosts of the ships' crews. Drowns people to serve him as slaves, but also protects fishermen who appease him by giving him the first fish of their catch. Likes butter and tobacco.

Also likes the rusalka, and often either marries one or takes several as servants or concubines. Rusalki are spirits of women who are murdered or die by suicide in water—sometimes children who were drowned by their mothers. (See Woman in White.) The adult versions sing to seduce passersby or sailors, then draw them underwater to become their spirit lovers. Lore sometimes suggests vampiric qualities. Some rusalki will vanish if their deaths are avenged. Can also be dispelled if kept out of water long enough for her hair to dry completely. The child versions can be dispelled by baptism with holy water.

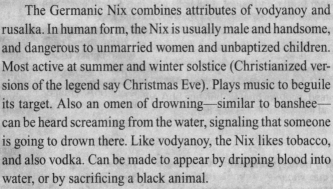

Have heard of vodyanoy from hunters in Alaska. Never seen one. Shoshone legends from Wyoming tell of Water Ghost Woman, who beguiles hunters and travelers with sexual attraction, also shoots them with spirit arrows.

The Germanic Nix combines attributes of vodyanoy and rusalka. In human form, the Nix is usually male and handsome, and dangerous to unmarried women and unbaptized children. Most active at summer and winter solstice (Christianized versions of the legend say Christmas Eve). Plays music to beguile its target. Also an omen of drowning—similar to banshee—can be heard screaming from the water, signaling that someone is going to drown there. Like vodyanoy, the Nix likes tobacco, and also vodka. Can be made to appear by dripping blood into water, or by sacrificing a black animal.

Once, in Pinckney, Michigan, I suckered a Nix by using a Black Shuck as the sacrifice. That was a show, a demon dog tangling with a water spirit. The Shuck won, and I sent it back to Hell for its trouble.

Sometimes the Nix appears as a horse called Bäckahästen, which, if ridden, will leap into the nearest body of water, drowning the rider. Overlap here with Celtic/Scottish stories of the kelpie and each uisge. Kelpies appear from the fog near rivers, and, if ridden, drown their riders. The each uisge can be ridden safely as long as it can't see or smell water. The minute it does, it drags the rider in and devours him, leaving only the liver.

This last detail I thought was just storyteller's elaboration until I tangled with an each uisge at the Quabbin Reservoir in Massachusetts. That one took human form, too, and looked like a handsome young man who always had weeds in his hair. I was lucky to get out with my liver.

I used to like swimming, but that's one more thing I lost to the job. Water spirits don't need much water, either. See British legends of Jenny Greenteeth or Peg-o'-the-Well. Egyptian El Nadaha ("the caller") lures children into canals to drown them.

Also have heard from other hunters about a haunted old racetrack in Goshen, NY. A horse and rider who drowned right after the turn of the century come back and ride across the lake, sometimes chasing or threatening people in the area. Bäckahästen, sounds like? But I haven't seen anywhere else that a human could be transformed into one.

November 2:

Mary has been dead for six years. Today I overheard the boys talking about her, about her death. Sammy's old enough now to be asking hard questions, and I think that's making Dean think about some things that he'd put away until now. He's a tough little kid, Dean. Like me. But he's also like me in the way he holds things in. Now his little brother is asking him things and he's got to figure out a way to protect Sammy while Sammy's questions put him through the emotional wringer all over again. And what do I do? They were talking to each other. If I butt in, they'll clam up. They've got the kid bond, the kind that keeps adults out. They'd tell me what I wanted to hear, but the truth is I can't get at the real way they feel about their mother, because I can't let them get at my feelings. It kills me every day. There's no way to tell them that. We have to go on and find whatever killed their mother, my wife. Mary.

For the boys' sake, I'm going to try to stay in one place for longer. Keep the hunting trips to a few hours' drive. At least until I have a firmer lead on what killed Mary. Then all bets are off.

1990

	DAY	NIGHT
1	Yain	Beron
2	Janor	Barol
3	Nasnia	Thami
4	Salla	Athar
5	Sadedali	Methon
6	Thamur	Rana
7	Ourer	Netos
8	Thamic	Tafrac
9	Neron	Sassur
10	Jayon	Agle
11	Abai	Calerva
12	Natalon	Salam

Spring: Caracasa, Core, Amatiel, Commissoros
Summer: Gargatel, Tariel, Gaviel
Fall: Tarquam, Guabarel
Winter: Amabael, Cetarari

January 24:

Dean turns eleven today. He asked for his own gun, and I got him one. A Seecamp LWS .32 automatic, the smallest gun I could find that offered any kind of stopping power. Dean and

64

I poured silver slugs for it ourselves, and we loaded it with alternating silver and Winchester hollow-points. He's got it in his pocket now.

May 2:

Sammy is seven today. I think we're going to get him through the first grade this year. He's a smart little kid, but we've moved around so much that he's a little behind in school. And I haven't been doing the stuff I need to do with him on that front. I need to be better about reading to him—stuff other than field manuals and weird newspaper headlines. He's okay at math, and he knows some scientific stuff, because he's seen people doing some weird experiments at the roadhouse and Pastor Jim's, but he needs your basic little kid school stuff. I'd ask Dean to do it, but there's only so much you can pile on a kid. Having Sammy's life in his hands is enough for Dean; he can't be responsible for home-schooling Sammy too. God. This is one more time I'm reminded how much we need Mary.

May 17:

This would have been our twelfth anniversary. Silk.

October 3:

Winstedt—Shaman, Saiva, and Sufi:

Sir Frank Swettenham has described how a spirit-raising séance was conducted by a royal female shaman during the illness of a ruler of Perak some thirty years ago. The magician, dressed like a man, sat with veiled head before a taper; in her right hand a sheaf of grass cut square at top and bottom. This sheaf she took convulsively.

The taper flared, a signal that the spirit invoked was entering the candle. The magician, now supposed to be in a trance, bowed to the taper "and to each male member of the reigning family present!" After many spirits had been invoked, the sick raja was brought out and seated on a sixteen-sided stand (an improvement on the double pentacle called Solomon's seat) to await, with shrouded head and a square bunch of grass in his hand, the advent of the spirits of the state. Conducted back to bed, His Highness fell later into a swoon attributed to possession by those spirits! At this royal séance the magician's daughter led an orchestra of "five or six girls holding native drums, instruments with a skin stretched over one side only" and beaten with the fingers.

In an account of yet another séance in Selangor, where to cure an ailment the magician became possessed by the tiger-spirit, it is said that the ceremony usually took place on three nights and that the same odd number of persons should be present each time. For the reception of the spirit an artificial bouquet of flowers, doves and centipedes, all made of palm-leaf, was prepared. After an invocation the magician bathed himself in incense, suffered spasmodic convulsions, spoke a spirit language, became possessed, sat with shrouded head, lit tapers on the edges of three jars of water, and rubbed the patient with a bezoar stone. Then donning a white coat and head-cloth, he fumigated a dagger, dropped silver coins into the three jars, and gazed to see their position under the three tapers, declaring that it indicated the gravity of the patient's illness. Scattering handfuls of charmed rice round the jars, he put into them improvised bouquets of areca-palm blossom, and plunged his dagger into each bouquet to dispel lurking spirits of evil. Another sheaf of palm-blossom he anointed with oil and used for stroking the patient from head to heel. Next he was possessed by the tiger-spirit, scratched, growled, and licked the naked body of the patient. He drew blood from his own arm with the point of his dagger and fenced with his invisible spirit foe. Once more he stroked the patient with the sheaf of blossom and with his hands. Again he stabbed the bouquets, stroked the patient, and after lying still for an interval recovered consciousness.

November 2:

Mary has been dead for seven years.

Psychopomp. Term for god or entity responsible for guiding souls to the afterlife. In Greece, Hermes. In Norse myth, the Valkyries. In Egypt, Anubis. Voodoo traditions, going back to their African roots, offer the Ghede. Irish, Ankou. In most shamanic traditions, the shaman is a sort of psychopomp both at the beginning of life and at the end. He or she was present at birth to usher the child into the world, and present at death to see the soul on its journey. Medieval legends of the scythe-bearing Grim Reaper perhaps connected to practice in some parts of Europe whereby the dead were stabbed or buried with sickles. The real reapers are purely psychic entities, with power over time and perception. They can change the way a human sees his surroundings, and change their own appearance, usually to ease the transition from life into death. The reaper's true form is hard to pin down, but most accounts suggest that *the natural way for a living person to see a reaper is as a wraith-like figure wearing tattered winding sheets or burial cloth.*

Black dogs are also psychopomps sometimes. Buried in the foundations of churches to guard and protect the gates between here and the afterlife.

December 25:

Battled a nasty little bugger today. Kicked the beast back to wherever it came from. But as I looked into that stinking mouth, I wondered for the hundredth time: when's my time gonna come? And if something happens to me, who'll take care of the boys? Dean tries to be the big man a lot, but he's not even twelve. And Sam's just seven. Just trying to do this without you is hard enough, Mary . . . Mary . . .

Mary . . .

Focus. The Beast of Bray Road. It's the Black Shuck and the hellhound all over again. Where do these black dogs come from? Agrippa had a black dog, said to be his familiar—he freed it from his deathbed and it trotted outside, never to be seen again. If you can believe anything anyone says about Agrippa. Even Churchill called his depression his black dog. What was really getting to him? He maybe needed a hunter around.

Some Christmas.

68

1991

DIDA'LATLI`'TÏ (To Destroy Life)

Sgë! Nâ'gwa tsûdantâ'gï tegû'nyatawâ'ilateli'ga.
Iyustï (O O) tsilastû''lï Iyu'stï (O O) ditsadâ'ita.
Tsûwatsi'la elawi'nï tsidâ'hïstani'ga. Tsû-
dantâgï elawi'nï tsidâ'hïstani'ga. Nû'nya
gû'nnage gûnyu'tlûntani'ga. Ä`nûwa'gï gû'nnage'
gûnyû'tlûntani'ga. Sûn'talu'ga gû'nnage
degû'nyanu'galû'ntani'ga, tsû'nanugâ'istï
nige'sûnna. Usûhi'yï nûnnnâ'hï wite'tsatanû'nûnsï
gûne'sâ gû'nnage asahalagï'. Tsûtû'neli'ga.
Elawâ'tï asa'halagï'a'dûnni'ga. Usïnuli'yu
Usûhi'yï gûltsâ'të digû'nnagesta'yï, elawâ'tï
gû'nnage tidâ'hïstï wa`yanu'galûntsi'ga. Gûne'sa
gû'nage sûntalu'ga gû'nnage gayu'tlûntani'ga.
Tsûdantâ'gï ûska'lûntsi'ga. Sa`ka'nï adûnni'ga.
Usû'hita atanis'se'tï, ayâ'lâtsi'sestï tsûdantâ'gï,
tsû'nanugâ'istï nige'sûnna. Sgë!

Mooney, Sacred Formulas of the Cherokee:
When the shaman wishes to destroy the life of another, either for his own purposes or for hire, he con-
ceals himself near the trail along which the victim is
likely to pass. When the doomed man appears the
shaman waits until he has gone by and then follows

69

him secretly until he chances to spit upon the ground. On coming up to the spot the shaman collects upon the end of a stick a little of the dust thus moistened with the victim's spittle. The possession of the man's spittle gives him power over the life of the man himself. Many ailments are said by the doctors to be due to the fact that some enemy has by this means "changed the spittle" of the patient and caused it to breed animals or sprout corn in the sick man's body. In the love charms also the lover always figuratively "takes the spittle" of the girl in order to fix her affections upon himself. The same idea in regard to spittle is found in European folk medicine.

The shaman then puts the clay thus moistened into a tube consisting of a joint of the Kanesâ'la or wild parsnip, a poisonous plant of considerable importance in life-conjuring ceremonies. He also puts into the tube seven earthworms beaten into a paste, and several splinters from a tree which has been struck by lightning. The idea in regard to the worms is not quite clear, but it may be that they are expected to devour the soul of the victim, as earthworms are supposed to feed upon dead bodies, or perhaps it is thought that from their burrowing habits they may serve to hollow out a grave for the soul under the earth, the quarter to which the shaman consigns it. In other similar ceremonies the dirt-dauber wasp or the stinging ant is buried in the same manner in order that it may kill the soul, as these are said to kill other more powerful insects by their poisonous sting or bite. The wood of a tree struck by lightning is also a potent spell for both good and evil and is used in many formulas of various kinds.

Having prepared the tube, the shaman goes into the forest, to a tree which has been struck by lightning. At its base he digs a hole, in the bottom of which he puts a large yellow stone slab. He then puts in the tube, together with seven yellow pebbles, fills in the earth, and finally builds a fire over the spot to destroy all traces of his work. The yellow stones are probably chosen as the next best substitute for black stones, which are not always easy to find. The formula mentions "black rock," black being the emblem of death, while yellow typifies trouble. The shaman and his employer fast until after the ceremony.

If the ceremony has been properly carried out, the victim becomes blue, that is, he feels the effects in himself at once, and, unless he employs the countercharms of some more powerful shaman, his soul begins to shrivel up and dwindle, and within seven days he is dead.

January 3:

Something new yesterday. I took out a nest of succubi—at least that's what everyone I talked to says they were. Sexually predatory, voracious demons. They can change their appearance, and they all transformed to look like Mary at one point. God help me, I was weak. It was like seeing her there again, in the flesh, and I let myself believe for just a minute. Or not believe, really. I agreed to their deception. And then, when I'd gotten my head straight again, I killed them. All of them. Was going to stay here for a while, but I think we'll need to be on our way. I'm going to stay in the West. Maybe New Mexico next, so we would be close to Daniel. I'm learning a lot from him, even though I've still never seen a vampire.

Succubi exist across world mythologies. Judeo-Christian versions have them as female demons who harvest semen that incubi (male version) then use to impregnate women with children who are more readily possessed by demons—or who are more likely to become witches. Birth defects were also said to be the result of incubi. A parallel European tradition, of the night-mare, is a creature which rides the sleeper, partially suffocating him and at the same time causing sexual dreams. The four succubi named in the Zohar are Naamah, Lilith, Elsheth Zenunim, and Agrat Bat Mahlat. Naamah was regarded as the inventor of divination, and in some traditions as a patron spirit of music.

In certain strains of Hebrew myth, incubi and succubi are generally called lilin and lilith. They are said to be the children of Lilith, and to die at a rate of one hundred per day because she would not come back to Adam. They can prey on children—boys until circumcision at eight days, and girls for twenty days—but also attack women by causing infertility and difficult births, even miscarriages. Men become victims of the lilith by being ridden at night, the seed being used to create more demonic children.

An amulet inscribed with the initials of the three Magi—Caspar, Melchior, and Balthasar—is said to protect children from lilin and lilith.

Other traditions include Greek empusa, which attacked travelers but also drained their life force through intercourse, and Turkish Al Basti (which also kidnaps horses). Martin Luther referred to Melusine as a succubus, but she doesn't seem to fit the mold; Melusine is more of a swan-maiden/selkie/kitsune type.

The succubi I killed said something about having plans for the Winchesters. Guess they'll have to cancel those plans.

January 24:

Dean turns twelve today. School has started again, but we're going to move on. Next week, the Winchesters are going to be residents of Albuquerque. Dean's going to be a normal sixth grader for at least the next couple of months. He even talked about wanting to play baseball this spring, but I'm not sure he's serious. I think he's taking his cues from me, talking about everyday stuff when I try to keep us in one place. Then when we're on the road again, all he can talk about is hunting.

March 17:

In the last week, Sammy has played a sunbeam in the school play and I killed a demon inhabiting the body of an old woman. It knew something about the succubi, I think. We're being followed. Or are we? Am I getting paranoid? I have every reason to be, but it's something I have to guard against. The boys are doing well. Sammy's talking about doing a science project to enter in the fair next month. He's really taken to his teacher, Ms. Lyle, and she's encouraging him. Smart kid, Sammy. It was warm today, and the boys kicked a soccer ball around. That's one of the nice things about Albuquerque. I picked up a job working construction. Feels good to be punching a clock again, actually. The regular rhythm of it. Part of me needs that. I thought about going back to turning wrenches, but it didn't feel right. I think a lot of things died in Lawrence, and that dream was one of them.

April 1:

Monday, I walked away from another job, and my younger son almost was kidnapped by some kind of demon. Sammy qualified for the New Mexico Science Fair, and his teacher, Ms. Lyle, said she'd take him. Only she started to take him somewhere else. I don't know where, but I caught up to her at a crossroads. She would have killed me, and taken Sammy, but Dean came through. I don't have any words for how proud I am of him. His brother's under some kind of spell, there's a giant monster made out of train parts coming after me, and he has the presence of mind to find this journal and read the exorcism out of it. I almost lost both of my boys today. Ms. Lyle, or the thing calling itself Ms. Lyle, wanted Sammy for something. It reminds me of the variant stories about succubi/lamiae taking children, or killing children. And if I'm honest with myself, I have to take that train of thought all the way: the stories also say that succubi come to claim the children that have been fathered by incubi, which is ridiculous.

I still don't know what Ms. Lyle wanted. She just said Sam was special.

We're on the road again. How am I going to explain to Sammy that we're not going back to school? How am I going to explain Ms. Lyle?

To top it all off, I had to give Sammy a sharp lecture on not talking to strangers. While I was on the phone with Bobby, he just got out of the car and went up to a black Seville. I read him the riot act—Dean too, since he let it happen and it's his job to watch Sammy. All Sammy would say about it was that the guy wanted to know where we were going.

April 7:

In Sioux Falls to meet Bobby, boys along since it's not safe for them to be in Albuquerque anymore. Between the two of us, Bobby and I hashed out what's been going on with Ms. Lyle and the others. Bobby thinks I'm a fool for not wanting to believe that demons really exist, and he's not shy about telling me. Probably he's right. All the signs were there with Ms. Lyle. But if you buy demons, you have to buy Hell, and if you buy Hell, you have to buy Satan, which means you have to buy God, right? I can't sign on to one belief if it means I have to take the others. Only Bobby says that he's never run across a demon who's laid eyes on the Devil. Most demons apparently don't even believe he exists. The way Bobby put it is that demons are a lot like us where belief is concerned. I don't see it that way. If demons exist, they are nothing like us.

But I guess I think they do exist. And I think Ms. Lyle was one. I was in bed with her . . . that thing . . . and it was a demon. I let it trick me away from the mission. I let myself be led, I let myself be convinced that everything can be normal again, and it was all a tactic. She wanted something from me, and she thought she knew how to get it.

And she was almost right. I've been lonely since Mary . . . I wanted to be touched. Just contact. And looking back, it makes me sick.

Have been reading up on crossroads out of Bobby's library. There's a nearly universal folk-magic tradition that crossroads are gateways between worlds. Robert Johnson: "I went to the crossroads / trying to flag a ride." And then he writes "Hellhound on My Trail," too. Wonder if he knew something . . . plenty of stories that he sold his soul to the Devil, but people have been saying that about musicians since medieval times. Another medieval note: criminals and suicides used to be buried at crossroads. A sacrifice to the spirits that used those gateways?

Papa Legba in voodoo magic is the loa of crossroads. You go to him if you want to talk to the iwa, the gods (going back to Yoruba traditions). He is the gatekeeper, also perhaps a psychopomp—like Eshu (sometimes called Ellegua in the Yoruba/Lukumi, later Exu in Brazilian folk magic). Eshu is the patron of travelers, god of crossroads. He's also a trickster, sometimes a cruel one. Both Eshu and Papa Legba must be the first of any spirits invoked if a magical or divination ritual is going to work. His symbol, called a veve:

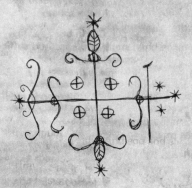

Veve is inscribed on the floor in some kind of powder. It can be anything from flour to gunpowder, depending on the ceremony. Hoodoo traditions prescribe certain actions at crossroads to gain gifts in music, love, or power. Or money.

April 18:

Went to see Silas last night. He's an old friend of Bobby's, some kind of soothsayer who sells tires. I went to his place and his daughter told me he's been in a coma . . . since last November 2, the seventh anniversary of Mary's death. When I went to see him at the hospital, he snapped out of it long enough to tell me a couple of things I didn't want to hear.

One, he thinks that Sammy's special somehow.

Two, Dean and I need to be ready "for what's to come."

Then he was gone again, out cold. What the hell does it mean? Why Sammy? What does he have to do with any of this? And what is coming? Silas either couldn't say anything else, or wouldn't. He said I brought him out of his coma, and then he was gone back into it.

Tomorrow I'm going to leave Sammy with Bobby so I can take Dean deer hunting. It's out of season, but the Dakotas are lousy with deer and Dean needs to pull a trigger to sharpen him up. Also I need to think about Sammy. Why was Ms. Lyle so interested in him?

More voodoo. The houngan (man) or mambo (woman) is the priest. You need them to talk to the loas, also called orisha (loas also known as iwa—African and New World terminologies mix freely). Orisha are said to be beings who manifest aspects of the natural world, and aspects of a nameless god. So they straddle the physical and spirit worlds. The bokor is a magician-priest who can do both divination/séance magic and darker magic: hexes, charms, etc. They're usually for hire. Bobby says that it's possible to be both houngan and bokor. Bokor are the ones who make zombies.

Ogun is the loa (or maybe iwa, or orisha?) of iron, smithy, hunting, fire, etc. He's a warrior. His veve:

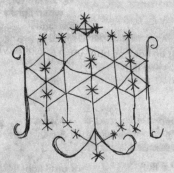

I've been hearing about a magical gun. The story goes that Samuel Colt one Halloween night made a gun and thirteen bullets that could kill anything. Wonder if that gun exists, or if it's just a hunter legend. And if it exists, I wonder where it is . . . Ogun would know. Tomorrow, after Dean and I go hunting, might be the time to ask him. Go to New Orleans? Must be a bokor down there who would do a hunter a favor.

Other veves:

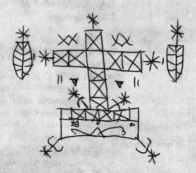

Baron Samedi, loa of the dead, stands at crossroads. Also loa of sex, known for his coarse appetites. Eros and Thanatos, all in one, dressed in tux and top hat. If you want to talk to him, bring plenty of booze and tobacco.

Maman Brigitte, Baron Samedi's wife, vulgar like her husband, likes to drink hot peppers. Protects gravestones if they are sanctified to her. She and Baron Samedi are related to the Ghede, a family of spirits that have to do with cemeteries, funerals, death, etc. Different traditions spell out the relationship differently. Either Samedi is a Ghede, or he created them or brought them to life, or he is an aspect of them and they speak through him.

I have to sleep. Up early tomorrow.

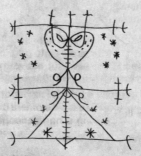

April 19:

The hunting trip was nearly a disaster. Dean missed his shot. I sent him after the buck, a beautiful twelve-pointer, and he dropped the gun when he tripped on the trail. Then out of nowhere comes Sammy, who picks up the gun and lays that big boy out. A seven-year-old . . . well, almost eight.

Then he tells me that he thought the deer had taken Dean's gun, and that Sammy had to protect him.

It's moments like those that kill me. I taught him that, Dean too. I taught them that everything should be seen as a threat. And now Sammy sees a deer and thinks it's trying to hurt his brother.

God.

Things got worse from there because Sammy told me he'd gotten up, wanting to come after me and Dean, and found the man in the black Seville outside Bobby's house. He rode in the Seville to the trailhead, and found us from there. I don't even know how to get my head around that. I feel like I should punish him somehow, but the truth is I should be punishing myself.

We get home, and Bobby tells me to go see Silas again. I didn't want to do it, but when I got to his house, there he was, awake and standing in his front door like he'd never been sick in his life. I don't know how to explain it. He said again that Sammy was special, and he wanted some time to talk to Sam and understand what was happening. So Dean and I left for an hour, and on the way back I saw the Seville.

When we got to Silas' place, there was Sammy, sitting on the porch. He said he and Silas talked for a while. I went inside, left Dean out with his brother to catch up. Inside . . . I've never seen anything like it. Or if I have, it was after an artillery strike in Nam. Silas was just in pieces, little bits of him stuck to the walls and the floor. Scrawled in blood on the kitchen cabinets, the words KILL HIM.

Now I've got to find the sonofabitch that killed Silas, too.

April 20:

Been on the run, running harder even than usual. The driver of the Seville called himself Anderson, said he was a hunter . . . and he was hunting Sam. He said Sam had killed Silas, but there's no way that can be true. No little boy could have done what I saw in there. But Anderson wouldn't listen, and now in the last twenty-four hours I've committed kidnapping, grand theft auto (well, semi), and murder. That's five hunters I've killed, if you count H—but who really knows what he was? And I don't know that Anderson was what he said he was, either. He passed up two chances to take Sammy out. I didn't give him a third. And I didn't give any of three Dowry brothers a chance at all.

It was Dean who killed Anderson. My oldest son is blooded. All I ever write about is death. Because all I ever see is death, and you know what? I did that to myself. It's got to end, but it can't end until I settle what happened to Mary.

May 2:

Sammy is eight years old today. Happy birthday, kiddo. No matter what the demons and soothsayers and lunatic albinos say, you're special to me just because you're my son. And I'm never going to let anything happen to you.

Ms. Lyle was after Sammy because he has something she wants. She said he was special. So did Silas. What's different about him? He's just a boy. My boy.

Have started reading about demonology because of Bobby.

I still have a hard time believing it. So far I'm sorting through a couple of different books that he says are important.

A New and Complete Illustration of the Occult Sciences (OS)

Written by Ebenezer Sibly. Fourth volume in a series begun 1784 and mostly dedicated to astrology. A disciple of Swedenborg and Mesmer. Makes liberal use of Reginald Scot's Discoverie of Witchcraft and Agrippa's De Occulta Philosophia.

Pseudomonarchia Daemonum (PD)

Written by Johann Weyer, 1563, from a book he calls Liber officiorum spirituum, seu Liber dictus Empto. Salomonis, de principibus & regibus dæmoniorum (note reference to Solomon here and in Weyes's subtitle: "Salomon's Notes of Conjuration"). Weyer a student of Agrippa. The Pseudomonarchia has much in common with the first book of the Lemegeton, called Goetia. A lengthy catalog of demons, with variations on their names, notes on their appearances, and brief instructions on conjuration and abjuration. Translated into English prior to 1584 by Reginald Scot as part of his Discoverie of Witchcraft. Full of odd notes about how many legions each demon controls, etc. Most of this isn't useful, but the characteristics of individual demons shed some light on the quest.

Goetia has better diagrams, and is more useful for actual conjuration.

The Testament of Solomon (TS)

Probably written 1st-4th century C.E. In Solomon's voice, tells of the building of the Temple and of the binding of numerous demons to perform menial labor. Several

of these demons not attested in other sources. The story goes on to tell how Solomon fell in love with a Jebusaean woman (Shunammite?) and desired her for a wife, but was told by the priests of Moloch that he could not have her unless he sacrificed five grasshoppers to Moloch. In a moment of weakness, he did, and fell away from God, becoming "the sport of idols and demons."

One of dozens of texts that characterize Solomon as an arch-magician. Queen of Sheba characterized as a witch, unlike her presentation in the <u>OT</u>. Also interesting that the Koran refers to the tradition that Solomon built the Temple with the assistance of bound demons: see sura 21, 34, 38.

<u>PD</u>, in its entry on Gaap, says that Solomon wrote a book of conjurations, and "mingled therewithal all the holy names of God."

May 17:

This would have been our thirteenth anniversary. Lace. Eleven is steel, twelve and thirteen are silk and lace? Feels like it should be the other way around, that steel should come later. Or maybe once you've proven you've got the steel to keep a marriage going, then you get to enjoy the silk and lace.

I'll never know.

November 2:

Mary has been dead for eight years. I've been learning about reapers. There's more than one, and it's not always a hooded skeleton with a scythe, but that's where I'll start. The traditional Grim Reaper is a skeleton or solemn-looking man carrying a scythe, who cuts off people's lives as though he were harvesting grain. Death personified is a figure or fictional character which has existed in mythology and popular culture since the earliest days of storytelling. Because the reality of death has had a substantial influence on the human psyche and the development of civilization as a whole, the personification of Death as a living, sentient entity is a concept that has existed in all known societies since the beginnings of recorded history. In the United States, Death is usually shown as a skeletal figure wearing a midnight-black gown with a hood, while in Europe he is often depicted similarly but dressed in white, which is the traditional color worn at funerals in many places.

Examples of death personified are:

- In modern-day European-based folklore, Death is known as the Grim Reaper or the Grim Spectre of Death.
- In Islam, Death is portrayed as Azrael, the angel of death (note that the name "Azrael" does not appear in any versions of either the Bible or the Koran).
- Father Time is sometimes said to be Death.
- Psychopomp is a spirit, deity, or other being whose task

is to conduct the souls of the recently dead into the afterlife.

In Ugaritic Mot "Death" (spelled mt) is personified as a god of death. The word is cognate with forms meaning "death" in other Semitic languages: with Hebrew ("moth" or "maveth"); with Canaanite, Egyptian Aramaic, Nabataean, and Palmyrene ("mut"); with Jewish Aramaic, Christian Palestinian Aramaic, and Samaritan ("mut"); with Syriac "maat"?; with Mandaean "muta"; with Akkadian "m'tu"; with Arabic "maut"; with Ge'ez "mot". Although Semitic languages aren't closely related to Indo-European languages, the words for "death" in Sanskrit ("mrit") and Latin ("mortus") are similar.

Mot (Death), son of 'El, according to instructions given by the god Hadad (Ba'al) to his messengers, lives in hmry (Mirey), a pit is his throne, and Filth is the land of his heritage. But Ba'al warns them:

> that you not come near to divine Death,
> lest me made you like a lamb in his mouth,
> (and) you both be carried away like a kid in the
> breach of his windpipe.

Hadad seems to be urging that Mot come to his feast and submit himself to Hadad.

Death sends back a message that his appetite is that of lions in the wilderness, like the longing of dolphins in the sea, and he threatens to devour Ba'al himself. In a subsequent passage Death seemingly makes good his threat, or at least is deceived into believing he has slain Ba'al. Numerous gaps in the text make this portion of the tale obscure. Then Ba'al/ Hadad's sister, the warrior goddess 'Anat, comes upon Mot, seizes him, splits him with a blade, winnows him in sieve, burns him in a fire, grinds him between millstones, and throws what remains on the field for the birds to devour. But after seven years Death returns, seeking vengeance for the splitting, burning, grinding, and winnowing, and demanding one of Ba'al's brothers to feed upon. A gap in the text is followed by Mot complaining that Ba'al has given Mot his own brothers to eat, the sons of his mother to consume. A single combat between the two breaks out until Shapsh (Sun) upbraids Mot, informing him that his own father 'El will turn against him and overturn his throne if he continues. Mot concedes and the conflict ends. In Sanchuniathon also Death is son of 'El and counted as a god, as the text says in speaking of 'El/Cronus:

> . . . and not long afterward he consecrated after his death another of his sons, called Muth, whom he had by Rhea; this (Muth) the Phoenicians esteem the same as Thanatos ["Death"] and Pluto.

But earlier in a philosophical creation myth Sanchuniathon has referred to great Wind which merged with its parents and that connection was called Eros (Desire):

> From its connection Mot was produced, which some say is mud, and others a putrescence of water compound; and out of this came every germ of creation, and the generation of the universe. So there were certain animals which had no sensation, and out of them

grew intelligent animals which were called "Zophasemin," that is "observers of heaven"; and they were formed like the shape of an egg. Also Mot bust forth into light, and sun, and moon, and stars, and the great constellations.

The language here is confusing, a
bad summary and possibly corrupt,
and the form "Mot" here is not
the same as "Muth," which appears
later. But it may be that the full and coherent
account would have made clear that muddy and putrescent
Death is the source of life.

<u>Putting God on Trial—The Biblical Book of Job: A Biblical
Reworking of the Combat Motif Between Mot and Ba'al.</u>

December 25:

Sometimes I think Sammy's been reading this journal.

But he's not going to read it tonight, because here we are, Christmas night, and there's two hundred miles of scrub prairie and desert between me and them. No Christmas tree, no carrots and milk for Santa and the reindeer. A couple of days ago I handed them presents, and they gave me a set of night-vision goggles that Dean must have pinched from a gun show we passed through in Amarillo a couple of months ago. They're growing up without me. And they're both starting to act out a little, because we're apart so much. Sam gets resentful and has some trouble handling his temper. Dean tries to fix everything and keep us together as a team. Neither of them should have to do those things.

After this year . . . the succubi and Ms. Lyle (Lilith?), Silas . . . this has been a rough one. They came after my boys. We made it, but they're going to keep coming. This enemy doesn't quit until they're dead, and I don't even know who's sending them. How do I fight them?

And how do I avoid this question: Would the boys be better off somewhere else, with someone else, living normal lives?

No. I'm their father. They belong with me.

Merry Christmas, everyone.

1992

January 24:

Dean turns thirteen today. For his birthday we went out to dinner at a greasy spoon called Mama Janer's, in Flint, Michigan. It's freezing and miserable here, and we're headed farther north to check out some things I've been hearing about shapeshifters in the North Woods, from Michigan all the way across through Minnesota. Odd for them to be active this time of year, since there aren't that many people outside for them to prey on. It makes me think something big is happening.

Outside L'Anse, in a roadhouse full of Indians from the lumber camp down the way, I overheard this:

There was a white woman named Jennie who had an Indian working for her—a shiftless, lazy Sioux. She hated him so much that if he was at the table, she wouldn't sit down, but he bragged down around the docks that he was going to have her. All I have to do, he said, is go into the woods and find the right root, and you'll see. I'll have that Jennie. Well, all of his buddies down at the docks, they made fun of him, but pretty soon he started leaving little candies around the table, and Jennie would eat them when he wasn't around so he wouldn't know she was doing it, and wouldn't you know it, all of a sudden—wasn't but a couple of months later—she up and married him. Then, when he had her in his power, he treated her real bad, almost starved her to death.

He worked his bearwalk on one of her relatives, too, and that was enough. They took care of him, and we didn't ever see him around here no more.

March 30:

I thought the lesson was learned back in Wisconsin, but the same thing almost happened again. I left the boys next at the beach in Two Lakes State Park and went looking for a skinwalker, and then it was Ichi all over again. Only this time the skinwalker took on the appearance of a park ranger it had killed, and nearly got the boys to come with it because they trusted the uniform. I still can't completely trust them on a hunt. I took it down, and lit into the two of them. Especially Dean. I have to be hard on him because one of these days I'm not going to be around, and he's the one who's going to have to look out for his brother. He's a badass, though. I thought I was tough when I was thirteen, but Dean would have kicked my ass six ways to Sunday.

April 27:

Procopius, Secret History, *on Justinian:*

And some of those who have been with Justinian at the palace late at night, men who were pure of spirit, have thought they saw a strange demoniac form taking his place. One man said that the Emperor suddenly rose from his throne and walked about, and

89

indeed he was never wont to remain sitting for long, and immediately Justinian's head vanished, while the rest of his body seemed to ebb and flow; whereat the beholder stood aghast and fearful, wondering if his eyes were deceiving him. But presently he perceived the vanished head filling out and joining the body again as strangely as it had left it.

Another said he stood beside the Emperor as he sat, and all of a sudden the face changed into a shapeless mass of flesh, with neither eyebrows nor eyes in their proper places, nor any other distinguishing feature; and after a time the natural appearance of his countenance returned. I write these instances not as one who saw them myself, but heard them from men who were positive they had seen these strange occurrences at the time.

They also say that a certain monk, very dear to God, at the instance of those who dwelt with him in the desert went to Constantinople to beg for mercy to his neighbors who had been outraged beyond endurance. And when he arrived there, he forthwith secured an audience with the Emperor; but just as he was about to enter his apartment, he stopped short as his feet were on the threshold, and suddenly stepped backward. Whereupon the eunuch escorting him, and others who were present, importuned him to go ahead. But he answered not a word; and like a man who has had a stroke staggered back to his lodging. And when some followed to ask why he acted thus, they say he distinctly declared he saw the King of the Devils sitting on the throne in the palace, and he did not care to meet or ask any favor of him.

May 2:

Sammy is nine years old today. Last year on his birthday we were getting the hell out of Albuquerque. This year I nearly lost the boys because of the skinwalker. They're both learning, but they've got a lot still to learn.

May 11:

This list is beings that can change their shape at will, or who undergo recurrent changes.

WEREWOLF (loup-garou, rougarou, oboroten, vrykolakas, pricolici, maj-coh): Change caused by full moon, or isolation, or brought on by recitation of a spell. Too many variations, and I've never seen one. Never met anyone who has, either. Needs some separate research. Lycaon?

VAMPIRE—ask Elkins

KITSUNE: Japanese fox spirit, has as many as nine tails to signify its age and wisdom. Can be tricksters, lovers, messengers of Inari. Myobu designates kitsune associated with Inari (kami of rice, color white); nogitsune are the variety that are untamed, tricksterish, dangerous. After living 1000 years, kitsune acquires its ninth tail along with the ability to see and hear anything happening anywhere in the world. They hate dogs, and the presence of a dog sometimes makes them revert when they have assumed human form. Often change appearance to beautiful young women, encountered alone. They will take human lovers, and bear children, but vanish again when their true nature is discovered. Also can appear in dreams. Kitsunetsuki is the term for possession by a kitsune, which causes the sufferer to behave like a fox and speak strange languages. Exorcism must take place in a shrine to Inari. Kitsune often carry round balls alight with kitsune-bi, foxfire. A human who gets one of these balls has leverage over the kitsune. As tricksters, kitsune often target pride and greed, taking people down a peg. Sometimes they're just malevolent, but this is rare. More likely to find them in abandoned houses, where they will resist new residents. Korean version known as kumiho, Chinese huli jing. Kumiho generally are evil, eating either human hearts or livers in an effort to consume human essence and become human themselves; less common variant stories have the kumiho becoming human by resisting its urge to kill for a thousand days. Huli jing more ambivalent, like kitsune. Emphasis in Chinese tales on possession and seduction.

TANUKI, Japanese "raccoon dog," can assume any shape and often takes on the appearance of inanimate objects—teakettles, etc.—to play a trick on humans. Largely good-humored, but can turn dangerous as well. Known for the size of their testicles. Very fond of alcohol, and like to play games with merchants by cheating them using disguised leaves as money.

BOUDA: East African were-hyena, from name of tribe where the power originated. Handed down matrilineally, power also related to more general witchcraft. (Witchcraft in Africa often related to blacksmiths . . . interesting. Think of Ogun and the Colt . .) Parallel were-hyena legend is of the qora. Ethiopian Jews often accused of being bouda. Also numerous legends in Ethiopia and Sudan that white—or albino—people had hyena blood, or could transform into hyenas.

WERE-JAGUAR (runa-uturungu in Argentina, also yaguarete-aba; chacmool in Mexico?)

SELKIE: Said to be souls of drowned people now inhabiting bodies of seals. Shed their seal skins to come ashore at prescribed intervals, or when they fall in love. If a human captures the skin, the selkie is in his (or, less often, her) power. Selkies live human lives, have human children . . . until they discover where their skin has been hidden. Then they seize it and return to the ocean. Some selkies are out to avenge hunting of seals—they are said to curse and sabotage fishermen. Tales come from across the North Atlantic, some similar stories in Pacific Northwest. Related stories of swan-maiden (swanmay, dove-girl, peacock maiden), various other animal-wife tales.

LESZY: Slavic woodland spirit, protector of forests and natural world. Tall men, with beards of grass and vines. Can assume any form, including plants and trees. Known to appear as a giant talking mushroom, and to keep company with wolves and bears. When in human form, his eyes glow green and his shoes are on the wrong feet. Will enter pacts with peasants or farmers, keeping their cattle or sheep from getting lost, but will also react violently to any perceived threat. Hides axes, leads lumberjacks astray, destroys signs, kidnaps young women, even known to tickle people to death. Leszy can be repelled by wearing clothes inside out or by starting a fire in their forests. Unusual among shape-shifting beings because it has a family: leszachka, wife, and leshonky, children.

NAGA: Common to Indian and Buddhist myth, nagas are snake spirits. Sometimes take human form to live among humans. More often they live in bodies of water or underground, where they guard treasure. Nagas have influence over natural events, and are offered sacrifices.

93

Worshipped across south and southeast Asia, from India to Tibet to Cambodia and all the way to Malaysia.

RAKSHASA: Reincarnated from evil human beings. Rakshasas are powerful shape-changers who may not have a native form. They also have magical powers, including invisibility. They are cannibalistic, and particularly target anything religious or holy. In addition to human flesh, they will eat spoiled food. Their fingernails are poisonous. In the <u>Mahabharata</u>, some rakshasas who give up cannibalism eventually become allies of humans.

YUXA: In Tatar folklore, a snake who reaches 100 years of age becomes a yuxa, and will assume the appearance of a young woman to have children, who then become more yuxa.

TENGU: Spirits of the arrogant or vain, tengu appear as old men or birds. Sometimes they attack those who are the most like they were in life—typically overly proud samurai, priests, nobles. More broadly, they deceive travelers, kidnap children, and lead priests astray. Often their victims are found tied to the tops of trees, sometimes insane. They have strong powers of illusion, and will possess young women in an attempt to seduce priests and monks away from their vows. If the tengu's identity is guessed or discovered, it has to assume its true form—a large bird, like a kite—and it will flee. Sometimes it can be propitiated with sacrifices. Usually in these cases a tengu has chosen a place to guard or make its home, and intruders who don't observe the proper rites are in for trouble.

PUCA: May appear as a variety of animals, always dark in color. Most often a horse who will give unexpecting humans

94

a wild ride. Can speak, and if it takes a liking to a person, it will give him advice—especially on November 1. Crops left in the fields after this date are considered to belong to it, as it is always hungry. If not fed, its temperament can turn more dangerous.

EACH UISGE: Usually a horse, can be a young man. As a human, tries to seduce young women. As horse, it carries its rider into the water before eating the rider, leaving only the liver. If kept away from water, it can be controlled.

ENCANTADOS: Group of beings from Brazilian lore. Can be snakes or disembodied spirits, but typically used to describe dolphins who can assume human form. Encantados come from another world, have magical abilities related to music and seduction. Like Celtic faeries, they sometimes kidnap children, especially progeny of their human liaisons—but no changeling stories. Encantados are known to drive people mad, but rarely kill outright. Will sometimes force a transmutation of a human into a new encantado, or simply glamour a human into following the encantado to its realm, known as Encante. In human form, they wear hats to cover their blowholes, which do not disappear in the transformation. A magical powder composed of manioc and chile, scattered over the water where the encantado appeared, is said to break their spell.

Loki-tricksters always can change shape? Ellegua, Coyote. Hell, Bugs Bunny is always dressing up like a woman . . .

May 17:
This would have been our fourteenth anniversary. Ivory.

June 21:

Last night, Sammy woke up in the middle of the night telling me he was afraid of the thing in the closet. I went and looked. There was nothing in the closet, but I've seen too much not to believe that there could be. So I handed Sammy the .45 and told him the next time he saw the thing in the closet, he knew what to do. I don't think I'll win any awards from parenting organizations, but five nights running now Sammy has slept without nightmares. Sometimes a .45 under your pillow is all you need.

Daniel says vampires can't change their shapes. Says that's all an invention of Bram Stoker.

November 2:

Mary has been dead for nine years. Nine years I've been on this quest, and I've accumulated so much stuff I needed to rent a storage space for it.

Omnes angeli, boni et mali, ex virtute naturali habent potestatem transmutandi corpora nostra.

All angels, good and bad, have the power of transforming our bodies.

December 9:

It is well known to all, that there is a Certain vertue in the Loadstone, by which it attracts Iron, and that the Diamond doth by its presence take away that vertue of the Loadstone: so also Amber, and jeat rubbed, and warmed draw a straw to them, and the Stone Asbestus being once fired is never, or scarce extinguished: a Carbuncle shines in the dark, the Stone Aetites put above the young fruit of Women, or Plants, strengthens them, but being put under, causeth abortion; the Jasper stencheth blood; the litle fish Echeneis stops the ships: Rhubarb expels choller; the liver of the Camelion burnt, raiseth showers, and thunders. The Stone Heliotrope dazles the sight, and makes him that wears it to be invisible, the Stone Lyucurius takes away delusions from before the eyes, the perfume of the Stone Lypparis cals forth all the beasts, the Stone Synochitis brings up infernal Ghosts, the Stone Anachitis makes the images of the Gods appear. The Ennecis put under them that dream, causeth Oracles.—Agrippa

Magus: Then there is the pyrophilus, of a red mixture, which Albertus Magnus reports that Æsculapius makes mention of in one of his epistles to Octavius Cæsar, saying, "There is a certain poison, so intensely cold, which preserves the heart of man, being taken out, from burning; so that if it be put into the fire for any time, it is turned into a stone, which stone is called pyrophilus."

1993

January 3:

Whether Scripture was read, or prayers were said,
Is more than the writer remembers;
But it runs in his head, ere the two went to bed,
They carefully covered the embers.

Yea, even much more—they locked every door
Upon horses, cows, heifers and stirks;
The house-doors were barred and the gateways tarred,
Thus, showing their faith in their works.

What more could be done? Smith loaded his gun
With powder and ball and with shot;
"Near the head of my bed I'll have it," he said,
"And for witches and thieves make it hot."

Gun loaded and cocked and all the doors locked,
Let witches and thieves do their best,
Gates bolted and barred, and some even tarred,
Man and beast might slumber and rest.

Folk magic among Pennsylvania Dutch known as
"pow-wow."

"Trotter Head, I forbid thee my house and premises; I forbid thee my horse and cow-stable; I forbid thee my bedstead, that thou mayest not breathe upon me; breathe into some other house, until thou hast ascended every hill, until thou hast counted every fence-post, and until thou hast crossed every water. And thus dear day may come again into my house, in the name of God the Father, the Son, and the Holy Ghost. Amen."

Written charm against evil spirits:

ı.

N. ı. R.

ı.

SANCTUS SPIRITUS

ı.

N. ı. R.

ı.

All this be guarded here in time, and there in eternity. Amen.

January 24:

Dean turns fourteen today. He took off to the movies with a girlfriend. I think her name is Katie. Quite the ladykiller, that kid. Like I was at his age. Hell-raising, foul-mouthed, full of piss and vinegar. Silas had it right: he's like me. If I'm not careful with him, by the time he's twenty he'll have left a trail of kids and arrest warrants all over the country.

April 19:

Davidians. Koresh from David and Cyrus. Cyrus the only
gentile given the designation "messiah" in the Tanakh. Thomas
Jefferson consulted Xenophon's biography of Cyrus when
drafting Declaration of Independence—April 19 also Lexington
and Concord. Also birthday of Eliot Ness.

May 2:

Sammy is ten years old today. It was a lousy day, for him and
me. He's on a soccer team, and he's pretty good, and today
was a game day. But it's only a game, and on Saturdays we
always do some kind of shooting now that they're both big
enough. Today it was bowhunting. Nothing's in season, so we
were just going target shooting, but it's important. They need
to know everything, every way to kill the enemy that's out
there. For Christ's sake, there are demons after Sammy. He
needs to know how to fight them, and Dean needs to know
how to protect him. Sammy's a kid, though, and he wants to
play soccer. He's even more stubborn than I am when he really
decides to dig in his heels. But I'm their father, and we went
out with the bows. I can't blame him for wanting a normal life,
but I wouldn't be much of a dad if I didn't prepare them for the
world they're living in. Doing what's right for your kids doesn't
always mean doing what they want. Especially in my case.

May 15:

Tulpa created through intense ritual visualizations known as
dubthab. Variation known as dragpoi dubthab is specifically
aimed at creating a thoughtform with the idea of harming another person. Physical form of tulpa becomes apparent to the
senses after the mind can begin to sense its spirit presence.

Tulpa thus created, no matter the creator's intent, will gradually turn on the creator.

Evans-Wentz wrote that enlightened magicians can destroy tulpa as easily as create them—also that those masters can incorporate their spiritual being into the body of another person. It's about the willpower.

Determined will is the beginning of all magical operations. . . . It is because men do not perfectly imagine and believe the result that the arts (of magic) are uncertain, while they might be perfectly certain.—Paracelsus

Related to atus in the Qliphoth?

All things are possible to him that believeth—Mark 9:23

Tulpas the idea behind urban legends? We tell each other stories, and when enough people are concentrating on an idea, or start to believe it, it becomes real . . .

गि लिगि र ड ढ ए ९ ढ ३ ६ ३ ४
ध द म र्ड र्झ ई ध ८ ३ द ५
र थ ॠ ३ ६ ष शि णु शि ॐ

May 17:

This would have been our fifteenth anniversary. Crystal. Crystal balls, divination, prisms . . . I want to talk to her so bad. Mary, why don't I dream about you anymore?

September 5:

Written charm carried by King Charles I, written by Pope Leo IX:

Who that beareth it upon him shall not dread his en-
emies, to be overcome, nor with no manner of poison
be hurt, nor in no need misfortune, nor with no thun-
der he shall not be smitten nor lightning, or in no fire
be burnt soddainly, nor in no water be drowned. Nor
he shall not die without shrift, nor with theeves to be
taken. Also he shall have no wrong neuther of Lord
or Lady. This be in the names of God and Christ †
Messias † Sother † Emannell † Saibaoth †

November 2:

Mary has been dead for ten years. Ten years. Been thinking about urban legends all year, and about how what happened at our house ten years ago might already be an urban legend in Lawrence, to go with Stull Church and the Eldridge Hotel. I've been a little crazy this past ten years, and on this day somehow it's easier for me to take a step back and look at how crazy I am. Ten years later, I still wake up wanting revenge. But this year I'm thinking about the vision of Mary I saw at Jim's, just a few weeks after she died. Whenever I think about that, I start wondering how I might see her again, talk to her. Truth is, I'm scared to try because of what happened at Jim's—and also because everything I read about séances talks about how dangerous they are, how easy it is for the séance to be a gate for something evil to come along with the spirit you want to contact. So I hold myself back.

Here's irony for you. Today I was reading some old urban legends, and meant to write this one down.

Bloody Mary: Chant "Bloody Mary" three times into a mirror in a dark room and her spirit will appear. Either it will kill you, gouge your eyes out, or mutilate your face. Why the hell would anyone do this? In a couple of variations she will prophesy for you. Other variations say to chant her name thirteen times. Historically, Bloody Mary was a nickname for Mary I of England, who suffered several miscarriages. More recent versions of the origin story say Mary was a witch who was either hanged or burned at the stake—or that she was mangled in a car crash—or that she killed her children, or had them taken from her, and committed suicide. Sometimes these variant stories come with different invocations: "Bloody Mary, I killed your baby" goes with the stories in which she is a grieving mother, "I believe in Mary Worth" with the version in which she was wrongfully accused of witchcraft or infanticide, and "Bloody Mary, I have your baby" those in which her children were taken from her.

Divination by mirror has been practiced in nearly all cultures for as long as mirrors have been around. Before that, any reflective surface, especially still water, was used to prophesy or catch a glimpse of the future. Aztecs created tezcatlipoca, "smoking mirrors," out of mercury poured into a bowl. Queen Elizabeth I's court magician, John Dee, prophesied with mirrors. Folklore from various places holds that if you perform a certain ritual while looking in a mirror, you will see your future husband. Eating an apple, brushing your hair, conducting any one of a thousand "wise woman" domestic rituals. A variation on this is looking into a well at sunrise to watch what reflection emerges as the light starts to shine into the well. In many of these stories, the danger is that you might also see some aspect of Death, which means you will die before marrying.

Tradition also holds that at the moment of a death, all of the mirrors in a house should be covered so they don't trap the departing spirit. Ancient Greeks and Indians believed that the reflection contained the soul, and could be captured by water spirits. Various South Pacific (Andaman, Motumotu) and African (Zulu, Basuto) traditions also hold that the soul is in the reflection, and is vulnerable when reflected. Basutos believe crocodiles try to take these souls.

It's bad luck to break mirrors because they're reflections of the soul, but also because they hold the future. That's why the seven years of bad luck. You've broken your future.

November 28:

Variation on Bloody Mary. I heard a hunter from Alabama say that in Camp Hill, on Loveladies Bridge, if you chant "Lovelady, Lovelady, I got your baby!" three times, you'll see the ghost of a woman who died with her children in a car accident.

Hookman: Teenagers parked in some lovers' lane somewhere, they're about to get things going when a news bulletin on the radio warns of an escaped convict with a hook for a hand. The girl suddenly isn't in the mood anymore, and the frustrated boy guns the car away. When they get home, there's a hook hanging from one of the door handles. An alternate version has the boy getting out to investigate, and the girl stays in the car all night, hearing strange noises, only to discover in the morning that her boyfriend has been murdered and is hanging in a tree above the car. Sometimes the strange noises are the sound of the dead boyfriend's fingernails scraping on the car roof. There

104

are plenty of real stories of lovers' lane murders—Son of Sam, case in Arkansas in 1946, others . . . story may have originated in Maine as early as the 1920s.

Vanishing hitchhiker: Outlines of this one are always the same. Late at night, someone picks up a young woman, sometimes a girl. Usually she's wearing white. She asks to be taken home, and doesn't say much else. Then, when the driver arrives at the address she's given, the backseat is empty. When the driver asks the people living at the address, he is told that the girl he describes died—or was buried—a few years ago near the same stretch of road where he picked her up. Lots of variations.

- The driver, wondering what happens to the coat he lent the girl, finds it draped over her tombstone
- Instead of hearing the story from the family, the driver sees a picture of the girl in the house and realizes what happened
- The hitchhiker tells the driver something about the future— often in these cases the hitchhiker is a nun
- The hitchhiker leaves something behind in the car, typically a scarf or purse

History of the vanishing hitchhiker goes back a long way. Joan Petri Klint wrote about a prophetic hitchhiker in Sweden in 1602. She changes beer to malt, acorns, and blood, then prophesies about harvests and war before disappearing. Other variations recorded since—18th-century English ballad called "A Suffolk Wonder," Washington Irving's story "The Lady with the Velvet Collar." Songs by Country Joe McDonald, Dickie Lee, Blackmore's Night, the Country Gentlemen. I remember the Dickie Lee song from the radio when I was a kid.

December 25:

Christmas in Joplin, Missouri. The boys got me a book that they must have stolen from a shop while I was rooting around in the esoteric shelves. Some other version of me, out there in a world where schoolteachers don't turn into demons, might have been able to raise the boys without turning them into thieves. But for us, it's a necessary evil. I try to discourage them from taking things we don't need. Anyway, it's an old book on theosophy. All the hunters I know are convinced that Blavatsky was a fraud, but I'll take a look at it. You never know where you're going to find a clue.

December 31:

Witch bottle: small glass bottle or flask specially prepared to trap spells or evil spirits. Contents typically included urine, hair, nail clippings, red thread. Larger stoneware vessels popularly known as Bellarmines, after a Catholic inquisitor. These were made with bearded faces, à la church gargoyles, intended to scare away evil. Bottles might also contain special earth, sea water, nails or pins, menstrual blood, thorns. Generally buried under the floor in a difficult spot to access—below the hearth or fireplace, sometimes threshold.

Cats sometimes also hidden in walls, also horse skulls. Folklore of both is that they would ward away familiars or see things that humans can't. Powerful wards. Sometimes shoes also used as spell traps, concealed within walls or floors.

Apotropaic: combating hostile magic, charms.

1994

January 24:

Dean turns fifteen today. A week ago he helped me take out a spirit haunting a grocery owned by an Indian family in Erie, Pennsylvania. It was like any other spirit—you find the remains, you salt, you burn. But also it wasn't. I'm learning that all spirits have some things in common, but it matters who they're haunting. It matters what their traditions were when they were alive. Have been reading about Indian mythology. Gods upon gods, thousands of them, and each of them has attendant monsters and demons. Some of the ones that keep popping up, not so much mythology as folklore, are pishacha and acheri.

Pishacha eat human flesh and are supposed to be the sons of anger. They haunt cemeteries and places where cremations have taken place. They can change their shape, and in some stories they can also become invisible. Sometimes they attack and eat their vicims, other times they possess them and drive them insane. I'm reminded of the unnamed demon in the *Testament of Solomon* who creeps "beside the men who pass along among the tombs, and in untimely season I assume the form of the dead; and if I catch any one, I at once destroy him with my sword. But if I cannot destroy him, I cause him to be possessed with a demon."

Acheri is a demon that disguises itself as a little girl. From Indian folk tradition. Acheri are said to inhabit the mountains and murder travelers who are taken in by its helpless guise. A protection against them is to wear a red thread around the neck (this was also said to protect small children against sorcery in some European countries).

Red thread: Kabbalah? According to the rabbis, there's no mention in the Torah or Talmud about red strings, also no mention in written Kabbalah. But an old folk superstition states that tying a red string around the body is a segulah, a protective act. Some Orthodox Jews tie red strings on the cribs of infants to ward off evil spirits or the evil eye. Scholarly Jewish tradition considers the red string a superstition that veers dangerously close to impiety, even idol-worship.

Sefer Yetzirah: Everything derived from the Word, the creation of language, from which comes every aspect of physical world. Seven pairs of contrasts:

> *There were formed seven double letters, Beth, Gimel, Daleth, Kaph, Pe, Resh, Tau, each has two voices, either aspirated or softened. These are the foundations of Life, Peace, Riches, Beauty or Reputation, Wisdom, Fruitfulness, and Power. These are double, because their opposites take part in life; opposed to Life is Death; to Peace, War; to Riches, Poverty; to Beauty or Reputation, Deformity or Disrepute; to Wisdom, Ignorance; to Fruitfulness, Sterility; to Power, Slavery.*

No good, no evil. The way a man lives his life in relationship to natural and divine order dictates whether he will perceive good or evil.

Tree of Life described in Sefer Yetzirah, but more in Zohar—belief among esoteric theologians that it corresponds with Tree of Life mentioned in Genesis. Two versions. One has

10 Sephirot, 22 connections; the other 11 and 24. Individual characteristics of Sephirot and pathways hotly contested.

Above the first Sephirah, Keter, is the Ayn Sof Aur, the beginning point that no mind can comprehend but that we need to grant so that there can be a beginning point. With Keter, Binah, Chakhmah, time and space begin. These are the Crown, Wisdom, and Understanding—rest of creation comes from these.

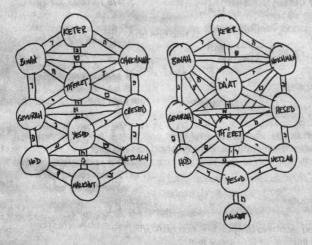

Tetragrammaton arranged in different ways can be tetraktys, as in Pythagorean mysticism. From tetraktys, quincunx was derived. Pythagoras also always used the pentagram with two points upward—this considered evil by medieval scholars/alchemists/demonologists.

May 2:

Sammy is eleven years old today. When Dean turned eleven, he wanted a gun of his own. Sammy asked me for a computer. That right there tells you all you need to know about the differences between them. I got him his computer, too. A Macintosh Performa. It's in the trunk right now, but every time we spend a night under a roof he's going to want it plugged in, I can tell. He was telling me about the Internet today. I'm not sure I understand what he's talking about, but according to Sammy, everything you could ever want to know is on the Internet somewhere, and if you have a computer you can find it. Looks like Team Winchester just took a big leap ahead when it comes to gathering information. Every army needs intelligence. We subscribed to Prodigy, which, according to Sammy, is the best way to get to the World Wide Web. I used one of the credit cards Bobby helped me get.

May 17:

This would have been our sixteenth anniversary. No traditional gift, or substance. Except in England, it's tungsten. Tungsten? How is that romantic?

October 31:

Witches known to change into rabbits, cats, other familiar animals. Halloween costumes a surviving remnant of the belief that transformed witches would be abroad before All Hallows' Eve . . .

George Gifford, 1608: In good sooth, I may tell it to you as to my friend, when I go but into my closet I am afraid, for I see now and then a hare, which by my conscience giveth me is a witch or some witch's spirit, she stareth so upon me. And—There is a foule great cat sometimes in my barne which I have no liking unto.

—A Dialogue of Witches and Witchcraft

Nahuales: Shamans who acquire the power to shape-shift. Name is Nahuatl (Aztec, originally nahualli in the plural), stories span Aztec, Maya mythologies and descendants—Mixtec, Zapotec, Tzeltal, so on. Each nahual has a tonal, animal aspect related to the day of the nahual's birth. The nahual can assume this shape, but often others as well. Some nahual have vampiric qualities, changing into bats or owls to drain blood; in other cases the nahual is a respected and feared member of a community, relied on to settle disputes. In some places nahuales are said to attack Indians who have too much contact with mestizo or Anglo populations. Montezuma's advisor Nezahualcoyotl said to be able to change shape, possibly escaped Cortez this way? Tradition persists parallel to brujeria, which has parallels in both European-style witchcraft and shamanism.

North America—Mohawk limikkin, "skinwalkers." Navajo version is yenaldooshi, who break a taboo to acquire magical powers. This taboo generally said to be murdering a relative. Once this is done, the yenaldooshi can change shape, although he goes in human form in ordinary circumstances. He will wear a coyote skin. The yenaldooshi attacks in two ways: it sprinkles a toxic powder made from corpses, which causes lingering and ultimately fatal sickness, and it uses a blowgun to shoot a small pellet of bone into the victim's body. This also causes a sickness that will eventually kill the victim. Yenaldooshi known to move through settlements at night, desecrating religious places.

Africa—Hausa witches I was telling Jim about a couple of years back. Can change into dogs.

Possibly related to Abraxas, or Abrasax. Collin de Plancy: "A god in certain Asian theogonies. From his name is derived the magical word Abracadabra. He is represented on amulets as having the head of a cock, the feet of a dragon, and a whip in his hand. Demonologists have made him a demon with the head of a king and with serpents for his legs. The Egyptian Basilides, 2nd-century heretics, looked upon him as their supreme god. Finding that the seven Greek letters contained in his name amounted to 365, the number of days in the year, they placed at his command several spirits who presided over the 365 heavens and to whom they attributed 365 virtues, one for each day. The Basilides also said that Jesus Christ, Our Savior, was but a benevolent spirit sent to earth by Abrasax." —Dictionnaire Infernal, 1863

Basilides a Gnostic sect. Other sources deny connection with Basilides, suggest Abraxas/Abrasax is a demiurgic figure syncretized from Jewish and other obscure tradition.

November 2:

Mary has been dead for eleven years. Eleven: doubled 1, said to represent a strand of DNA. Also balance. Prime number. First number you can't count on your hands. Eleventh of the major arcana is Justice.

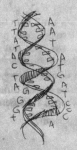

Revelations 11:11: "And after three days and a half the Spirit of life from God entered into them, and they stood upon their feet; and great fear fell upon them which saw them."

December 11:

WENDIGO

Cree: Evil that devours. Half phantom, half man, half beast. Wood spirit, very thing. Cannibal/magic. Eats live flesh. Lives in forests.

Perfect hunter: heightened senses, speed, strength, power. Enhanced vision, smell. Cunning and insane. Not bound by moral restrictions nor conventional restraints. With superhuman abilities, lives by instincts as an animal. Ferocious, ravenous, evil. Strength of wild animal, freedom to roam forest, hunt for live meat. Eats only living flesh.

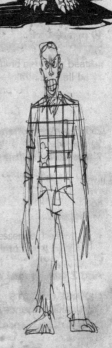

Wendigo knows how to fast long winters—hibernates for years at a time—will hunt when necessary. Legends from local lore state that it's hundreds of years old—was once a man, and turned into cannibal, possibly from conditions such as harsh winters cut off from supplies. Miner/hunter/courier DeBois: conditions of isolation & depravity turned him into a monster. Different cultures around the world carry similar legends. Cannibalism

113

endows the consumer with certain powers such as heightened senses, strength, speed, agility.

Desperate, lonely—what price survival? Eats members of his own tribe. Always hungry, alone, numb. Less than human. Can never return, senses gone in normal sense. Wendigos are feared in history—petroglyphs are clear depictions—North American versions: gigantic spirit, over fifteen feet tall, glowing eyes, long yellow fangs, overly long tongue, most have yellowish sallow skin. Some are matted with hair, lanky, and driven by hunger. Can be male or female, but always hungry. Some versions of the legend have them growing in size with every meal, so there's always more to feed. Others say wendigo has a heart of ice which must be shattered or melted to kill it.

Cannibalism plus magic equals a dark, dark road. I've never seen anything so hungry. Every motion and sound and breath of the wendigo is about hunger. It's stealthy when stalking its prey, blinding fast when pouncing, savage and ravenous when eating.

I wish I didn't know about that last part, but you see things in this job.

Algernon Blackwood didn't know the half of it.

SACRED SYMBOL
SOUTHWEST AMERICA
UNIVERSAL SYMBOL
OF 7TH SUN, FOUR
DIRECTIONS, FOUR WINDS

THE SEEING EYE
POWERFUL SYMBOL FOR
SIGHT AND DIVINATION

THE THREE RAY
SUN SYMBOL OF
LIFE ENERGY
AND POTENTIAL TO HEAL

THE WIND ELEMENT AND
CHEVRON OF LUTE STRING
TALISMAN TO CALL UPON
THE NATURAL ELEMENTS
FOR PROTECTION & HELP

THE SPRING SUN
TENDERNESS AND
GOODNESS PROTECTOR

SACRED SYMBOL SNOW
AND THE POWER OF THE
COLOR WHITE ALSO THE
POWER OF THE WINTER SUN

THE PROTECTION
AGAINST BEASTS
AND PHANTOMS

Sacred Symbol ORIG.
Aganda came fire NORTH
AMERICA TO MU-SHAMU
by the inscription on the
tablets RETURN TO THE
DARKNESS

THE MIDDAY SUN
A SYMBOL OF
TRANSITION
AND POWER

INTERNAL LIGHT AND
STRENGTH, INNER
FORTITUDE & WISDOM

RISING SUN
SACRED SYMBOL
TO WARM & PROTECT

SACRED SYMBOL OF MAN
POWERFUL DEPICTION TO
HELP AND TO INDICATE
BENEFICENT PRESENCE

POWER SUN
SACRED SYMBOL
PROTECTION &
GUIDANCE FOR
TOWARD OF
DARKNESS

LITTLE COLORADO PETRO
SYMBOL OF MAN AND
STRENGTH TO INDICATE
THE INHERENT INNER
STRENGTH WITH IN EACH

SUN RISE OVER
MOUNTAIN TO
INDICATE THE
COMING DAWN

SYMBOL OF SNAKE
COLORADO BASKET MAKER
ARCHEAO/ASTROLOGICAL

SPIRAL SACRED
SYMBOL OF
CONTINUUM
GOLDEN MEAN

ANASAZI SUN SYMBOL
TO BRING FORTH LIGHT
SACRED WHEEL OF LIFE
TO INDICATE CONTINUUM

014552.010 CARVED
SYMBOLS COLLECTED FROM CAVE 38, 101 TO 42, 152,
AND PAINTED COPIES

Monday, September 10
8 am
1
1
Noon
Tuesday, September 11
8 am
9
10
11
Noon
Wednesday, September 12
8 am
9
10
11
Noon

1 pm
1 pm
1 pm
1 pm

Total

014552.010 Carved and painted symbols
collected from Cave 38, 101104.2.152

1995

January 13:

Verstegan says werewolves "are certayne sorcerers, who having annoynted their bodies with an ointment which they make by the instinct of the devil, and putting on a certayne inchaunted girdle, does not only unto the view of others seem as wolves, but to their own thinking have both the shape and nature of wolves, so long as they wear the said girdle. And they do dispose themselves as very wolves, in worrying and killing, and most of humane creatures." Verstegan hints that the werewolf has no conscious memory of its actions while it is transformed—"to their own thinking." Other accounts, not Verstegan's, have this hand-in-hand with a belief that werewolves can only transform while they are asleep.

From Virgil:
Moeris for me these hearbs [herbs] in Pontus chose,
And curious drugs, for there great plenty grows;
I many times, with these, have Moeris spide [spied]

Chang'd to a wolfe, and in the woods to hide:
From Sepulchres would souls departed charm,
And Corn bear standing from anothers Farm.

January 24:

Dean turns sixteen today. We're in Montana, and I think we're on the trail of a werewolf. That bow-hunting practice is going to come in handy. Sometimes you can't use a gun, and this is one of them. Tomorrow we're going out on a hunt, and I'm going to let him take the lead.

January 25:

Bull's-eye. Dean is a helluva shot with anything. He's coming into his own as a hunter.

Werewolves will avoid wolfsbane when they can, as well as holy artifacts and silver. Being stabbed or cut with a silver knife can sometimes force a werewolf to revert to human shape. The silver bullet legend is probably true, but not all hunters believe in it. You hear grumbles around the gathering places. I was at the roadhouse not too long ago and heard three hunters complaining that either they'd done something wrong when they made their silver bullets, or that some werewolves just weren't affected.

Lycanthropy might have a cure. According to some traditions, killing a particular werewolf removes its curse on all those it's bitten—severing the bloodline, in a way.

He who desires to become an oborot, let him seek in the forest a hewn-down tree; let him stab it with a small copper knife, and walk round the tree, repeating the following incantation:

On the sea, on the ocean, on the island, on Bujan,
On the empty pasture gleams the moon, on an
    ashstock lying
In a green wood, in a gloomy vale.
Towards the stock wandereth a shaggy wolf,
Horned cattle seeking for his sharp white fangs;
But the wolf enters not the forest,
But the wolf dives not into the shadowy vale,
Moon, moon, gold-horned moon,
Check the flight of bullets, blunt the hunters' knives,
Break the shepherds' cudgels,
Cast wild fear upon all cattle,
On men, all creeping things,
That they may not catch the grey wolf,
That they may not rend his warm skin!
My word is binding, more binding than sleep,
More binding than the promise of a hero!

Then he springs thrice over the tree and runs into
the forest, transformed into a wolf.

My master had gone to Capua to sell some old clothes. I seized the opportunity, and persuaded our guest to bear me company about five miles out of town; for he was a soldier, and as bold as death. We set out about cockcrow, and the moon shone bright as day, when, coming among some monuments, my man began to converse with the stars, whilst I jogged along singing and counting them. Presently I looked back after him, and saw him strip and lay his clothes by the side of the road. My heart was in my mouth in an instant, I stood like a corpse; when, in a crack, he was turned into a wolf. Don't think I'm joking: I would not tell you a lie for the finest fortune in the world.

But to continue: after he was turned into a wolf, he set up a howl and made straight for the woods. At first I did not know whether I was on my head or my heels; but at last going to take up his clothes, I found them turned into stone. The sweat streamed from me, and I never expected to get over it. Melissa began to wonder why I walked so late. "Had you come a little sooner," she said, "you might at least have lent us a hand; for a wolf broke into the farm and has butchered all our cattle; but though he got off, it was no laughing matter for him, for a servant of ours ran him through with a pike. Hearing this I could not close an eye; but as soon as it was daylight, I ran home like a pedlar that has been eased of his pack. Coming to the place where the clothes had been turned into stone, I saw nothing but a pool of blood; and when I got home, I found my soldier lying in bed, like an ox in a stall, and a surgeon dressing his neck. I saw at once that he was a fellow who could change his skin, and never after could I eat bread with him, no, not if you would have killed me. Those who would have taken a different view of the case are welcome to their opinion; if I tell you a lie, may your genii confound me!

From an old edition of the <u>Satyricon</u>

New World versions. Loup-garou known in Canada and places where French settled in U.S. Loup-garou legends from precolonial Illinois: after the initial transformation, a loup-garou was doomed to spend 101 days of nightly transformations, followed by days of melancholia and sickness. The only way to get out of the sentence early was if someone managed to draw blood from the loup-garou, and in this case, neither party involved could ever speak of the incident until the remainder of the 101 days had passed.

Variation called rougarou known in southern U.S.—in some versions said to be a crocodile after transformation, rather than a wolf. Crocodile transformations also known in Egypt and Indonesia. Often New World versions are said to become werewolves because of isolation and failure to observe religious practice, or because of some broken taboo. Cannibalism? One of the earliest werewolf legends is the story of Lycaon, transformed into a wolf after eating human flesh and trying to serve it to Zeus. Herodotus and Pliny also told of people turned into wolves. In the Bible, Nebuchadnezzar said to imagine himself as a wolf.

Throwing a piece of iron over a transformed werewolf is said to force it back into its human shape. Related to belief that faeries can't touch iron?

April 20:

Going to Oklahoma City. More than two people involved? Word already out among hunters that McVeigh had some questionable associates. Possible supernatural angle. Sightings in the area in days before explosion. Daniel says he's heard something about freak weather. 35° 28' N 97° 32' W

May 2:

Sammy is twelve years old today. He's a handful. Spends all of his time on the computer, unless he's arguing with me. I can't understand him, and he doesn't try to understand me. Typical father-son trouble, but it feels worse because neither one of us can talk about what happened to his mother. He wants to be in one place, live a normal life. The older he gets, the more he wants it. But the older he gets, the more I'm going to need him to help on the hunt. He's got to understand that. We will finish this quest, and he's going to be a part of it.

> *Behind the veil of all the hieratic and mystical allegories of ancient doctrines, behind the darkness and strange ordeals of all initiations, under the seal of all sacred writings, in the ruins of Nineveh or Thebes, on the crumbling stones of old temples and on the blackened visage of the Assyrian or Egyptian sphinx, in the monstrous or marvelous paintings which interpret to the faithful of India the inspired pages of the Vedas, in the cryptic emblems of our old books on alchemy, in the ceremonies practised at reception by all secret societies, there are found indications of a doctrine which is everywhere the same and everywhere carefully concealed.*
>
> —*Eliphas Levi, introduction to* Dogme et Rituel de la Haute Magie

May 17:

This would have been our seventeenth anniversary. If we'd been British, turquoise. But Americans don't believe in seventeenth anniversaries, I guess. And I never got to have one. Turquoise carv-

SUN ☉	SUN	GOLD	LION	GOLD
MOON ☽	MON	SILVER	CAT	SILVER
MARS ♂	TUES	IRON	WOLF	RED
MERCURY ☿	WED	MERCURY	APE	PURPLE
JUPITER ♃	THUR	TIN	HART	BLUE
VENUS ♀	FRI	COPPER	GOAT	GREEN
SATURN ♄	SAT	LEAD	MOLE	BLACK

ings placed in Native American graves to attract good spirits and guard the grave. Also, turquoise tied onto a bow was supposed to make you shoot more accurately.

Levi: "Superstition is the sign surviving the thought; it is the dead body of a religious rite."

Right mixture of the seven gives Electrum, per alchemists.

Gold	Au
Silver	Ag
Iron	Fe
Mercury	Hg
Tin	Sn
Copper	Cu
Lead	Pb

November 2:

Mary has been dead for twelve years. Biblical necromancy, from II Samuel:

7 Then said Saul unto his servants, Seek me a woman that hath a familiar spirit, that I may go to her, and enquire of her. And his servants said to him, Behold, there is a woman that hath a familiar spirit at Endor.

8 And Saul disguised himself, and put on other raiment, and he went, and two men with him, and they came to the woman by night: and he said, I pray thee, divine unto me by the familiar spirit, and bring me him up, whom I shall name unto thee.

9 And the woman said unto him, Behold, thou knowest what Saul hath done, how he hath cut off those that have familiar spirits, and the wizards, out of the land: wherefore then layest thou a snare for my life, to cause me to die?

10 And Saul sware to her by the LORD, saying, As the LORD liveth, there shall no punishment happen to thee for this thing.

11 Then said the woman, Whom shall I bring up unto thee? And he said, Bring me up Samuel.

12 And when the woman saw Samuel, she cried with
   a loud voice: and the woman spake to Saul, saying,
   Why hast thou deceived me? for thou art Saul.

13 And the king said unto her, Be not afraid: for
   what sawest thou? And the woman said unto
   Saul, I saw gods ascending out of the earth.

14 And he said unto her, What form is he of? And
   she said, An old man cometh up; and he is
   covered with a mantle. And Saul perceived that
   it was Samuel, and he stooped with his face to
   the ground, and bowed himself.

15 And Samuel said to Saul, Why hast thou
   disquieted me, to bring me up? And Saul
   answered, I am sore distressed; for the
   Philistines make war against me, and God is
   departed from me, and answereth me no more,
   neither by prophets, nor by dreams: therefore I
   have called thee, that thou mayest make known
   unto me what I shall do.

16 Then said Samuel, Wherefore then dost thou
   ask of me, seeing the LORD is departed from
   thee, and is become thine enemy?

Deuteronomy 18 also warns against divination
from the dead. Widely practiced in the ancient Near
East—Persia, Babylonia, Chaldea. King Herod also
thought that Jesus was John the Baptist brought
back to life by necromancers.

THE MAGUS, FRANCIS BARRETT

*Hence it is that the souls of the dead are not to be
called up without blood or by the application
of some part of their relict body. In the raising there-*

123

fore of these shadows, we are to perfume with new blood the bones of the dead, and with flesh, eggs, milk, honey, and oil, which furnish the soul with a medium apt to receive its body.

It is likewise to be understood, those who are desirous to raise any souls of the dead, ought to select those places wherein these kind of souls are most known to be conversant; or by some alliance alluring the souls into their forsaken bodies, or by some kind of affection in times past impressed in them in their life, drawing the souls to certain places, things, or persons; or by the forcible nature of some place fitted and prepared to purge or punish these souls: which places for the most part are to be known by the appearance of visions, nightly incursions, and apparitions.

Therefore the places most fitting for these things are church-yards. And better than them are those places devoted to the executions of criminal judgements; and better than these are those places where, of late years, there have been so great and so many public slaughters of men; and that place is still better than those where some dead carcass that came by violent death is not yet expiated, nor was lately buried; for the expiation of those places is likewise a holy rite duly to be adhibited to the burial of the bodies, and often prohibits the soul returning to its body, and expels the same afar off to the place of judgment.

Oil, from Exodus 30: Olive oil infused with cinnamon, calamus, cassia, and myrrh. Cinnamon: control. Calamus: binding other elements. Cassia: curative, protective. Myrrh: purification.

Oil of Abramelin: infused with cinnamon, myrrh, galangal Galbanum oil: in Liber Juratus—angels

November 13:

Sammy's soccer team won a division championship. On to the state playoffs. I'm proud as hell of him, and I'm sad too. He's battling to keep himself together the only way he knows how—by rebelling. Only because he's Sammy, he rebels toward being normal. I get it, even if I can't let it keep happening. We owe Mary too much to give up now. But I'm going to keep this trophy.

December 1:

Qliphoth originally described as that which separates the human from the divine design in the Tree of Life . . . or worldly residue of once-holy sparks of divine being. Later seen as evil or fallen versions of sephirot, or as necessary result of Adam and Eve eating of the Tree of Knowledge, creating an imbalance in the universe that was restored by creation of qliphoth. Diagram here expanded to incorporate ideas from medieval demonology. Qliphoth sometimes characterized as coming into being whenever sin or evil occurs, and manifesting as misfortune, disaster, or demonic entities.

Babylonian Talmud counts the number of demons as 7,405,926? Figure from Weir, *Pseudomnoarchia Daemonum*. 1111 x 6666. Doesn't divide evenly into 666. Or 616.

QLIPHOTH—MEDIEVAL VERSION

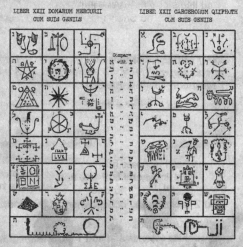

LIBER XXII DOMARUM MERCURII CUM SUIS GENIIS

LIBER XXII CARCERORUM QLIPHOTH CUM SUIS GENIIS

1996

January 24:

Dean turns seventeen today. We went shooting. Then I sent him out on his first hunt. I've let him take the lead before, but I've always been there to back him up. This time he's on his own. Partly it's a test, and partly I wanted some time with Sammy. Should be no problem for Dean. Ghosts of two nuns haunting St. Stephen's Indian Mission in Riverton, Wyoming. Simple salt-and-burn mission. Nuns in love with each other, then discovered. Killed themselves. We scoped the situation out, figured that something must be left behind that's now a focus for the haunting. Bible, rosary beads, some small article that's hidden somewhere in their room. I figured Dean would take care of it no problem, but I still stayed close by with Sammy.

The boys are old enough now that we can start spending a little more time in one place. Thinking California, maybe. When I need to fly solo, they're big enough to stay home by themselves for a while without me worrying. When we go on a hunt together, they can bring their homework. That's what I wanted to talk to Sammy about. It's going to be hard enough getting his bullheaded self through adolescence without also having to fight every other day about how he wants to be Jimmy Normal. We can make this work if we do it together—but he's going to have to know that everyone pulls their weight. Mary comes first.

Dean took care of the nuns just like I thought he would, but

I don't think I'm going to be sending him on any more solos soon. That one was a little tense.

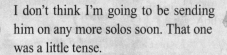

43° 32′ 9″ N 109° 38′ 9″ W

March 11:

Called Fossilman by the locals, but possibly Cannibal Owl? Oka-moo-bitch, Shoshone legend of being that would take bad children, and sometimes unwary hunters. Associated folklore of children learning magic or hunting while in Owl's captivity, sometimes learning to turn his tricks against him. Shoshone, Paute, Shuswap.

To Shoshone, petroglyph sites known as Poha Kahni, House of Power. Spirit world closer to the surface there. After ritual bath in a hot spring, the shaman went to Poha Kahni and entered a trance to journey in the spirit world and capture power, or return with knowledge or kidnapped souls.

May 2:

Sammy is thirteen today. He's finishing sixth grade, a year late and with all the grudges to show for it. When Dean hit this age, I started to worry about girls, booze, drugs . . . all the regular stuff. With Sammy, I don't worry about that. What worries me is that he's got so much bottled up inside him that when it comes out, he won't be able to control it. I think that's part of why he has the dreams. He's different, my Sammy. I think he's a little haunted by being in the room with Mary when she was killed. He feels like he should remember something, or be able to offer a clue. God, it must be terrible to know you witnessed something but that you'll never be able to remember it or tell anyone about it. I think he also wonders about Ms. Lyle. Dean and I never told him the whole story.

June 17:

Slave Hauntings, Lynching Sites:

CLINTON COURT, HELL'S KITCHEN, NY: Sailor known as Old Moor hanged there when it was a potter's field. Has haunted ever since. Blamed for at least two deaths since the field was built on, one in the 1820s when he scared a woman into falling down the stairs, another later, little girl, no details except might have also involved a fall.

HICKORY HILL, EQUALITY, IL: Quarters built for slaves leased into Illinois to work in a salt mine. Owner, J. H. Crenshaw, also kidnapped free blacks and sold them South. 1846, one of his slaves cut Crenshaw's leg off with an ax. Quarters riddled with spirits of slaves who died there. Hard to find all of their remains. Salt mine also likely haunted, but it's been closed for decades.

BECKER FARM, SELKIRK, NY: Now part of GE Plastics complex, farmhouse still standing. Becker caught his wife in the sack with a slave, killed them both, then hanged himself. GE quit using house after several mysterious events.

HENRY HUDSON PARK, GLENMONT, NY: Old slave quarters near the river off 9W. Four kids and a cop disappeared sometime in the early 1980s. No press coverage, nobody there will talk about it.

FLORENCE, AL: Runaway slaves hung from a bridge through the middle of town.

GENEVA, AL: Intersection of Pea River and Choctahatchee River. Tree once used for hangings, nothing will grow near it.

GADSDEN, AL: Crestwood Cemetery haunted by ghosts of murdered slaves from when it was a plantation. Ghostly packs of dogs have also been reported.

JACKSONVILLE, AL: Chief Ladiga Indian Trail. At the edge of an uncompleted subdivision, slave quarters in the woods. The area haunted by visions of hanging bodies and ghosts of slaves and lynch mobs.

MOBILE, AL: Oak tree growing behind the public library said to be over the unmarked grave of a wrongfully killed man who swore that the tree would grow to prove his innocence.

STEELE, AL: Settlement of freedmen burned by night riders after the Civil War. Their spirits still haunt the location.

CROSBY, TX: Neighborhood built over slave cemetery haunted by poltergeist activity.

AUGUSTA, GA: Pillar on Broad Street, where the old slave market used to be. Cursed by one of the sold slaves—anyone who has tried to damage or remove the pillar has died?

NEWMAN, GA: Northgate HS haunted by ghost of a slave lynched after he killed his master?

POCOMOKE FOREST, MD: Area said to be haunted by ghosts of children drowned because they were offspring of plantation owner raping his slaves.

MT. MISERY ROAD, NC: Stretch from Brunswick to Fayetteville haunted by spirits of slaves who died on the way from Cape Fear docks to market.

CAYCE, SC: Apartment complex on the site of a plantation haunted by ghosts of infants discarded in plantation outhouses.

That's it. I can't write these down anymore.

May 17:

This would have been our eighteenth anniversary. Bismuth. A brittle metal, silvery white with tinges of pink and other colors.

August 21:

> *From Agrippa: "And so we must understand that which Psellus the Platonist saith, viz. that Dogs, Crows, and Cocks conduce much to watchfulness: also the Nightingale, and Bat, and horn Owle, and in these the heart, head, and eyes especially. Therefore it is said, if any shall carry the heart of a Crow, or a Bat about him, he shall not sleep till he cast it away from him. The same doth the head of a Bat dryed, and bound to the right arme of him that is awake, for if it be put upon him when he is asleep, it is said, that he shall not be awaked till it be taken off from him. After the same manner doth a Frog, and an Owle make one talkative and of these specially the tongue, and heart; So the tongue also of a Water-frog laid under the head, makes a man speak in his sleep, and the heart of a scrich-Owle laid upon the left breast of a woman that is asleep is said to make her utter all her secrets. The same also the heart of the horn Owle is said to do, also the sewet of a Hare laid upon the breast of one that is asleep."*

November 2:

Mary has been dead for thirteen years. Longer than I knew her. What does it say about me that I've devoted more of my life to her death than I ever did to her life? If I could only see her again, just once, so I could ask her if she thinks I'm doing the right thing . . . but remember what happened at Jim's that first time. Would it be her? How would I know? Also remember Ms. Lyle.

Life is about remembering the dead and making sure you protect the living.

Met an alchemist who believes that the souls of the dead can be pinned into homunculi. Offered to do this for me and Mary. I turned him down, but it wasn't easy. Spirits that can't go on turn bad, and I couldn't stand to see that happen to her. I've seen it happen to too many other people who were loved.

November 14:

Got this one from one Emil Besetzny, who published a book in 1873 about homunculi created by John Ferdinand, Count of Kuffstein (if there wasn't a place called Kuffstein, someone would have to make it up), in about 1775. Besetzny's sources were apparently Masonic manuscripts and the journal of the count's butler, who went by the name of Kammerer. The count's collaborating alchemist was a Rosicrucian monk by the name of Abbé Geloni.

> *The bottles were closed with ox-bladders, and with a great magic seal (Solomon's seal?). The spirits swam about in those bottles, and were about one span long. . . . They were therefore buried under two cartloads of horse manure, and the pile daily sprinkled with a certain liquor, prepared with great trouble by the*

two adepts, and made out of some "very disgusting materials." . . . After the bottles were removed, the "spirits" had grown to be each one about one and a half span long, so that the bottles were almost too small to contain them, and the male homunculi had come into possession of heavy beards, and the nails of their fingers and toes had grown a great deal. . . . In the bottle of the red and in that of the blue spirit, however, there was nothing to be seen but "clear water"; but whenever the Abbé knocked three times at the seal upon the mouth of the bottles, speaking at the same time some Hebrew words, the water in the bottle began to turn blue (respectively, red), and the blue and the red spirits would show their faces, first very small, but growing in proportions until they attained the size of an ordinary human face. The face of the blue spirit was beautiful, like an angel, but the face of the red one bore a horrible expression.

Once every week the water had to be removed, and the bottles filled again with pure rainwater. This change had to be accomplished very rapidly, because during the few moments that the spirits were exposed to the air they closed their eyes, and seemed to become weak and unconscious, as if they were about to die. But the blue spirit was never fed, nor was the water changed; while the red one received once a week a thimbleful of fresh blood of some animal (chicken), and this blood disappeared in the water as soon as it was poured into it . . .

. . . the spirits gave prophecies about future events that usually proved to be correct. They knew the most secret things, but each of them was only acquainted with such things as belonged to his station; for in-

stance, the king could talk politics, the monk about religion, the miner about minerals & etc.; but the red and blue spirits seemed to know about everything.

By some accident the glass containing the monk fell one day upon the floor and was broken. The poor monk died after a few painful respirations, in spite of all the efforts of the count to save his life, and his body was buried in the garden. An attempt to generate another one, made by the count without the assistance of the Abbé, who had left, resulted in a failure, as it produced only a small thing like a leech, which had very little vitality and soon died.

And about golems: Most golems can't speak. Idea is that if granted speech, they would have a soul, and that an imperfect creation (created by man rather than God) would have an imperfect soul and be dangerous.

Sanhedrin 65b:
Rava stated: If they wish, Tzadikkim could create a world. Rava created a man and he sent it to Rabi Zeira. Rabi Zeira spoke with it and it did not respond. Rabi Zeira then stated, "You are created by my colleague, return to your dust." Rav Chanina and Rav Oshiah would sit every Friday and study the Sefer Yetzirah and create a calf that has reached a third of its potential development and subsequently eat it.

Eleazar of Worms mentions golems in commentary on Sefer Yetzirah:

Whoever studies Sefer Yetzirah has to purify himself, don white robes. It is forbidden to study alone, but

only in two's and three's, as it is written, . . . and the
beings they made in Haran (Gen. 12:5), and as it is
written, two are better than one (Eccl. 4:9), and as
it is written, it is not good for man to be alone; I will
make a fitting helper for him (Gen. 2:18). For this
reason Scripture begins with a "bet"—"Bereshit
bara," He created.

It is required that he take virgin soil from a place
in the mountain where none has plowed. Then he
shall knead the soil with living water and shall make
a body and begin to permutate the alef-bet of 221
gates, each limb separately, each limb with the cor-
responding letter mentioned in Sefer Yetzirah. And
the alef-bets shall be permutated first, then afterward
he shall permutate with the vowel—alef, bet, gimel,
dalet—and always the letter of the divine name with
them, and all the alef-bet. . . . Afterward he shall ap-
point bet and likewise gimel and each limb with the
letter designated to it. He shall do this when he is
pure. These are the 221 gates.

To control the golem, the creator writes one of the names
of God on its forehead, or on a tablet under its tongue. This can
then be erased or removed. Or the creator could write the word
Emet (אמת "truth") on its forehead. By erasing the first letter
in Emet to form Met (מת "dead") the creator would destroy
the golem.

According to Kabbalah, a golem can never disobey its
creator.

1997

January 7:

Detroit and Ypsilanti, Michigan, laid out by Augustus Brevoort Woodward. Magician, esoteric, Freemason. Both plans executed after fires: Detroit 1805, Ypsilanti 1825?

More lore picked up around the Wolverine State:

SNAKE GODDESS OF BELLE ISLE. Legend of Detroit-area Indians, from the Ottawa. Princess hidden in a covered canoe by the chief, her father. Her suitor discovers her and takes her to his wigwam, angering the winds, who beat him to death. Spirits help the chief hide her on

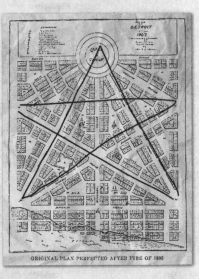

ORIGINAL PLAN PERFECTED AFTER FIRE OF 1805

Belle Isle, protecting her with snakes. She is sometimes seen as a white deer. The spirit of her unlucky lover is stuck on Peche Island. First European settlers in the area called Belle Isle Rattlesnake Island. Frequent sightings of a woman in a white gown (woman in white), as well as white deer.

NAIN ROUGE. Legend comes from Normandy, where the dwarf was a fisherman's helper—though sometimes a trickster too. In Detroit, the dwarf is dangerous. It is sometimes naked, sometimes wearing a ratty fur coat or fur boots. Has black hair, reddish skin, burning eyes, appears and disappears at will. Every appearance portends disaster for whoever sees it, and for the city. Appearances:

1701: Cadillac attacks it with a sword. Shortly after, he is financially ruined and his reputation wrecked. Forced to leave Detroit, goes first to New Orleans and then back to France.

1763: British soldiers see dwarf before the Battle of Bloody Run, where they are slaughtered by Pontiac.

1805: Dwarf seen immediately before the fire that destroys the city. Woodward then plans the rebuilding. Sightings in the smithy where the fire began.

1812: General Hull reports a dwarf attacking out of the fog after his failed attempt to cross the river and invade Canada. Surrenders the city to the British not knowing that he outnumbers them. Later court-martialed and sentenced to the firing squad. Sentence commuted.

1967: Multiple sightings of the dwarf before riots that start on 12th Street. Much of the city burns, riot accelerates decline of the area.

1976: Power-line workers see dwarf before ice storm.

Less reliable sightings in 1884, 1964.

REMARKABLE COINCIDENCE
INFANTS FALL TWICE ONTO SAME MAN

Joseph Figlock, a city street sweeper, has become an unwitting guardian angel to the offspring of this city's blithely fortunate young mothers. Last year, an infant fell onto Mr. Figlock as he was performing his duties in an alleyway. Figlock and the fortunate child were both slightly injured in the encounter. Last night, David Thomas, two years of age, fell from a fourth-story window, and again Figlock was there to break the child's fall.

January 24:

I gave Dean the Impala today for his eighteenth birthday. The car is 30 years old now, amazing it runs as well as it does. I've taught Dean a lot of what I know about working on cars, which was everything until 1983. Haven't kept up since then, all the computers and emissions spaghetti drives me nuts. Give me a fat 327, no electronics, just pistons, crankshaft, and a gas pedal. That's a car. And now it's my son's. He knows I'll still be driving it, but he's a man now, and since he's already made his share of kills, this was the only rite of passage I could think of. He goddamn well better take care of it.

February 23:

POLTERGEISTS

Lithobolia: or, the Stone-Throwing Devil. Being an Exact and True Account (by way of Journal) of the various Actions of Infernal Spirits, or (Devils Incarnate) Witches, or both; and the great Disturbance and Amazement they gave to George

<u>Waltons Family, at a place call'd Great Island in the Province
of New-Hantshire in New-England, chiefly in Throwing about
(by an Invisible hand) Stone, Bricks, and Brick-bats of all Sizes,
with several other things, as Hammers, Mauls, Iron-Crows,
Spits, and other Domestick Utensils, as came into their Hellish
Minds, and this for the space of a Quarter of a Year.</u>

Hell of a title. 1698 account by Richard Chamberlain
of 1682 haunting attributed to the neighbor being a witch.
No record of whether neighbor was tried. Other notable
American poltergeists—the Wizard of Livingston, Virginia,
1797; Bell Witch, Kentucky, 1817; Fox sisters, 1848, were a
hoax but initial events might be real.

Overlap with incubus/demonic possession in Entity and
Smurl cases, both in the 1970s.

Missouri says poltergeists are unquiet spirits, not psychokinetic
projections. They want attention, and if they don't get it they
progress from nuisance to danger. Only way to get rid of them
is the same way you get rid of any spirit. Find the remains, or
the haunted object, salt and burn, repeat as necessary.

April 28:

Heard from Bobby today. He and a group went up to some fly-
speck town in South Dakota because there were rumors about
demonic possession there. Looks like nothing happened.
The place was clean. I talked to Bobby for a long time about
demons. I'm starting to think that I don't have any choice but
to believe in them.

April 30:

Exorcism for an area or community. Takes the form of a prayer
to St. Michael the Archangel, which is kind of ironic because

there's no such thing as angels. Ask any hunter. Demons, now those are real. So when you call out to an angel that doesn't exist, what are you really calling out to? I don't know if I would trust this one.

St. Michael the Archangel, illustrious leader of the heavenly army, defend us in the battle against principalities and powers, against the rulers of the world of darkness and the spirit of wickedness in high places. Come to the rescue of mankind, whom God has made in His own image and likeness, and purchased from Satan's tyranny at so great a price. Holy Church venerates you as her patron and guardian. The Lord has entrusted to you the task of leading the souls of the redeemed to heavenly blessedness. Entreat the Lord of peace to cast Satan down under our feet, so as to keep him from further holding man captive and doing harm to the Church. Carry our prayers up to God's throne, that the mercy of the Lord may quickly come and lay hold of the beast, the serpent of old, Satan and his demons, casting him in chains into the abyss, so that he can no longer seduce the nations.

We cast you out, every unclean spirit, every satanic power, every onslaught of the infernal adversary, every legion, every diabolical group and sect, in the name and by the power of our Lord Jesus Christ. We command you, begone and fly far from the Church of God, from the souls made by God in His image and redeemed by the precious blood of the divine Lamb. No longer dare, cunning serpent, to deceive the human race, to persecute God's Church, to strike God's elect and to sift them as wheat. For the Most High God commands you, He to whom you once proudly presumed yourself equal; He who wills all men to be saved and come to the knowledge of truth. God the Father commands you. God the Son commands you. God the Holy Spirit commands you. Christ, the eternal Word of God made flesh, commands you, who humbled Himself, becoming obedient even unto death, to save our race from the perdition wrought by your envy; who founded His Church upon a firm rock, declaring that the gates of hell should never prevail against her, and that He would remain with her all days, even to the end of the world. The sacred mystery of the cross commands you, along with the power of all mysteries of Christian faith. The exalted Virgin Mary, Mother of God, commands you, who in her lowliness crushed your proud head from the first moment of her Immaculate Conception. The faith of the holy apostles Peter and Paul and the other apostles commands you. The blood of martyrs and the devout prayers of all holy men and women command you.

Therefore, accursed dragon and every diabolical legion, we adjure you by the living God, by the true God, by the holy God, by God, who so loved the world that He gave His only-begotten Son, that whoever believes in Him might not perish but have everlasting life; to cease deluding human creatures and filling them with the poison of everlasting damnation; to desist from harming the Church and hampering her freedom. Begone, Satan, father and master of lies, enemy of man's welfare. Give place to Christ, in whom you found none of your works. Give way to the one, holy, catholic, and apostolic Church, which Christ Himself purchased with His blood. Bow down before God's mighty hand, tremble and flee as we call on the holy and awesome name of Jesus, before whom the denizens of hell cower, to whom the heavenly Virtues and Powers and Dominations are subject, whom the Cherubim and Seraphim praise with unending cries as they sing: Holy, holy, holy, Lord God of Sabaoth.

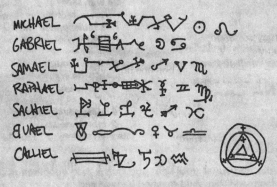

Four classes of demons in Judeo-Christian demonology, corresponding to cardinal directions and four elements. Also four seasons.

Waite, The Occult Sciences: *"Much that passed current in the west as White (i.e. permissible) Magic was only a disguised goeticism, and many of the resplendent angels invoked with divine rites reveal their cloven hoofs. It is not too much to say that a large majority of past psychological experiments were conducted to establish communication with demons, and that for unlawful purposes. The popular conceptions concerning the diabolical spheres, which have been all accredited by magic, may have been gross exaggerations of fact concerning rudimentary and perverse intelligences, but the wilful viciousness of the communicants is substantially untouched thereby."*

May 2:

Sammy is fourteen years old today. He's been having strange dreams again. I've tried to keep an eye out for any signs that he's more than a regular kid, but I don't see them. He's sensitive, has a lot of imagination, but that's about it. Plus now that he's hitting adolescence, he's a giant pain in the ass. Dean just chased girls and snuck around with beers in his coat pockets. That was teenage trouble I could understand. But Sammy just shuts down sometimes. Won't talk to anyone, and when he does, it's only because he wants to argue about something. He's got all the willpower us Winchesters are known for, but in him it sits quietly. You don't notice it's there until he decides he feels strongly enough about something that he won't compromise. Then you might as well wrestle angels.

May 10:

Quincunx. In hoodoo used to create a magical crossroads to increase potential of a spell. Known as a "five-spot." Fixes the components of a spell, and intensifies their power. Can also be used as a symbol around the outside of a property or location to ground the user's power and prevent malign influence. Basic pattern like the 5 on a die, variations more or less infinite. Sir Thomas Browne:

quincunx "a symbol of the quinta essentia which is identical with the Philosopher's Stone."

Quincunx sometimes incorporated into protective conjuration circle.

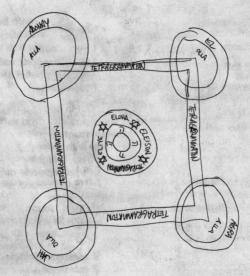

May 17:

This would have been our nineteenth anniversary. Nobody thinks nineteen is worth a traditional gift.

Number is sacred in Islam and Baha'i. 19 Arabic letters in the Basmala, 19 months of 19 days each in the Baha'i calendar. Solar eclipses tend to be 19 years apart. Babylonians considered the 19th day of every month to be unlucky.

May 23:

SAMUEL COLT

1814-1862. Born and died in Hartford, CT. One of seven children. Various revolver designs, first submitted for patent 1832? Same year Colt went on missionary trip to Calcutta.

The Colt: Made in 1835 for a hunter, during the appearance of Halley's Comet that year—perihelion November 16, Struve observations from August 20-November 16. Would have been visible from other parts of Earth for several weeks after. Colt created during this period(?). Descriptions of it make it sound like a Paterson, but it must be different somehow—Paterson fired cap-and-ball, and if Colt made 13 bullets—supposed to be numbered—they must be cartridges. Metal cartridges not introduced into Colts until 1873? Some retrofitted before that. A bullet fired from it will kill anything, even beings that normally don't die from bullets or any kind of physical damage. Everyone you talk to has a different story about how the Colt has been used. Nobody living has ever seen it, as far as I know. Standard manufacture of Paterson ran from 1836-1842—discontinued after that when company failed, although Colt's creditors sold Paterson models until 1847.

1835 Colt the first of its kind? Prototype, the Ur-Colt. Progenitor of all revolvers that followed. Not the first time a blacksmith or metalworker has tinkered with the occult. African orisha Ogun, god of iron, fire, war. Throughout western Africa, blacksmiths regarded as priests and magicians. Abyssinian/Ethiopian and Congo traditions hold that blacksmiths are magicians. Dactyls, Corybantes, Cabiri, Curetes, other ancient peoples considered magicians because of their prowess in ironworking, blacksmithing. Norse myth the same—Wieland, tale of Thord Vettir. German tradition that the blacksmith ends his work on Saturday by striking his anvil, chaining the Devil for another week. Blacksmiths also said to recognize gods and devils. In parts of the Slavic countries, oaths can be sworn on an anvil. From India and Scotland, stories that disease and demonic possession can be cured by the touch of an anvil or water from a smithy.

December 1, 1835. The date works, and it's the feast of St. Eloy, or Eligius, who is patron saint of blacksmiths and farriers. Eligius known for sending his servants and monks throughout southern France to take down the bodies of executed criminals and bury them with full rites—precaution against revenants?

Micah Jenkins born—Confederate general, killed by own men at Wilderness 5/6/64
Hans Christian Andersen publishes first book of fairy tales
Jacob Rome is born—Ohio congressman, mayor of Toledo

Could hunter have been David Crockett or Jim Bowie? Both explorers, both died at Alamo. Every story I hear about the Colt has something to do with the Alamo, but the siege didn't happen until 1836 . . . Crockett left for Texas on Halloween 1835. Halley's Comet would have been visible. Bowie already there, on December 1 he was searching for legendary Los Almagres mine.

June 3:
GOLDEN RATIO
Integral to pentagram. Shorter and longer sections of each line exist in golden ratio. Also expressed in nautilus spiral. Occurrences in nature: human ear approximates spiral. Ratio of feet to navel / navel to crown is golden ratio. Also elbow-wrist / wrist-fingertip.
Position of God's fingers in Michelangelo's fresco. Lindenmayer grammar.
1.618, approx.—Fibonacci numbers normalize around this ratio along a diminishing sine curve. Fibonacci popularized Hindu-Arabic numerals in Europe at the turn of the 13th century. Before, European mathematicians had used Roman numerals. Learned from Arab mathematicians in Algeria and elsewhere.

0　1　1　②　③　⑤　8　⑬　21　34　55　㊙　144
㉝　377　610　987　⑮⑨⑦　2584　4181　6765
10946　17711　㉘⑥⑤⑦　46368　75025　121393
196418　317811　⑤⑭⑨　832040　1346269

Final digits in Fibonacci series repeat themselves, cycle
length 60. Final two digits also, cycle length 300.

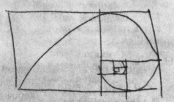

Five Platonic solids: tetrahedron, cube,
octahedron, dodecahedron, icosahedron. Also the
five basic Dungeons and Dragons dice, according to Sammy.

June 16:

Got one of my boys through school. Dean is graduated. Seems
like a miracle, after I don't know how many schools, but it
happened. He's got his diploma.

Looks like Sammy's going to take an extra year. He's just
going to be starting ninth grade next fall, because we were
moving so much when he was in second, third, fourth grades
that we lost a year and I don't think we'll be able to get it back.
I haven't talked to him about it, but he must know it's going to
happen. Couple of times I've tried to talk to school adminis-
trators about double-promoting him, but then they want to see
test scores, gifted enrollments, that kind of thing. I don't have
any of that. What I do have is a borderline-genius kid who's
going to be nineteen when he graduates high school.

July 24:

Tacitus on worship of Nerthus:

On an island in the sea stands an inviolate grove, in which, veiled with a cloth, is a chariot that none but the priest may touch. The priest can feel the presence of the goddess in this holy of holies, and attends her with deepest reverence as her chariot is drawn along by cows. Then follow days of rejoicing and merry-making in every place that she condescends to visit and sojourn in. No one goes to war, no one takes up arms; every iron object is locked away. . . . After that, the chariot, the vestments, and (believe it if you will) the goddess herself, are cleansed in a secluded lake. This service is performed by slaves who are immediately afterward drowned in the lake. (Germania)

Lindow Man, Tollund Man, Grauballe Man, Ramten, Bjeldskovdal, Bocksten, Gadevang, Yde, Soro, Bourtanger. UK, Germany, Denmark.

Early Romans buried slaves in building foundations. Akin to English practice of burying dogs, except slaves are people. Spirits? An entombed slave can't be a happy resident of the afterlife. Pre-Roman British evidence shows people buried in structures there. No wonder they needed witch bottles.

Foundation sacrifice. German and Celtic records, folktales include various mentions of people—often children—entombed in walls of castles or buildings. Sometimes in bridge pilings. From <u>Hessische Sagen</u>:

High water and ice on the Haun River so damaged a miller's spillway every winter that he was no longer able to raise the funds to repair it.

147

Dismayed, one day he was standing at the spill-way when he was approached by a drunkard who offered him advice. He promised to make the spillway so secure that it would never again be damaged, but the miller would have to pay him well.

The miller agreed, and the drunkard said, "Find a boy for us. We will bury him alive beneath the foundation stone, and I guarantee the durability of the spillway."

The miller shuddered, but when the drunkard offered to provide a boy for fifteen pecks of groats, he entered into the agreement, and forthwith they dug the grave.

The next day the child cried in vain. The two men pushed him into the pit, threw stones in on top of him, and soon the spillway was ready.

Soon thereafter the drunkard's corpse was pulled from the Haun River. The miller's conscience so gnawed at him that he wasted away and then died.

From that time forth the miller wanders about, attempting to pull passersby into the river. Every year he must lure at least one person into the river. Usually they are drunkards. He is on the lookout for them, because it was one of their kind who brought misfortune upon him.

Adds water spirit/curse to the foundation sacrifice story. Unquiet ghosts. Human sacrifice in London Bridge? Last verse of the rhyme: "What has this poor prisoner done?" Bones of saints were often interred in the cornerstones of cathedrals, so their spirits would guard the holy location. Unwilling sacrifices would be more likely to become angry spirits, haunting instead of guarding. Dante's <u>Commedia</u> refers to foundation sacrifice of Buondelmonte on Easter 1215.

> Ma conveniesi, a quella pietra scema
> che guarda 'l ponte, che Fiorenza fesse
> vittima ne la sua pace postrema.

Florence needed to offer a victim to the stone which guards the bridge—meaning the statue of Mars at the Ponte Vecchio. Sacrifice to the stone, and to Mars, sets the stage for Florence's troubles in the next century. Canaanites sacrificed infants and put them in foundations of houses and temples. Gezer, Megiddo, Ta' Annek. Joshua 6:26: "At the cost of his first-born shall he lay its foundation, and at the cost of his youngest son shall he set up its gates." Again in 1 Kings 16:34. In Europe, Copenhagen, Liebenstein, Slavensk, Granderkesse, Oldenberg, Rugby. Tlingit in Alaska sacrificed slaves or prisoners on the hearth of a new house.

Bones discovered in the basement of the farmhouse where Fox sisters started their séances. Also Hainesburg Viaduct, New Jersey.

Jimmy Hoffa?

August 22:

Michigan Dogman, lycanthrope? Sightings dating back to 1938, across northern Michigan. Some reports say the creature was threatening, others are typical Bigfoot-style cryptozoologist invention. Might be worth taking a look. Especially since that part of the country seems to breed sightings of dog/wolf creatures—Beast of Bray Road. Is the Dogman a shape-shifter? Werewolf? Or is it some kind of hellhound creature?

There's a song about it on local radio now, so every drunk idiot out in the woods is going to be seeing it for months ... but that doesn't account for sixty years of sightings. Trying to correlate missing persons and unsolved crimes with those sightings. Nothing yet.

1974-77
Janna Saari
Perry Corlew, Phil LaCroix, Gunter Foster
Evie Sadowski
Phyllis St. Pierre
Edouard Laurent
April Norman

Giordano Bruno, Zosimas of Palestine, Pseudo-Dionysus

November 2:

Mary has been dead for fourteen years.

Death is the separation of the soul from the body. The creation of a zombie is the rebinding of body and soul via necromancy. The animated body can move, speak, even think, but it still can't outrun physical decay. Zombies don't last very long, and the more able they are to think, the more they suffer from the same derangement that eventually gets any spirit that's been prevented from moving on. It's a rule: if spirits can't move on, the tug of the afterlife sooner or later drives them mad.

I guess this is all supposed to make me feel better about her being dead.

Agrippa: "In like manner they say, that a cloth that was about a dead Corpse hath received from thence the property of sadness, and melancholy; and that

> the halter wherewith a man was hanged hath certain
> wonderfull properties."

TRUTH ABOUT AMITYVILLE. INDIAN CURSE?

John Underhill, Massacusetts Indian fighter, massacred Massapequans near Amityville. Sachem, Takapausha, said to haunt the area, possessing individuals for revenge. Another local legend also holds that a spirit in Lake Ronkonkoma kills a couple every year because she died while running away with a lover forbidden to her. Drowning victims in Lake Ronkonkoma often disappear for months. Bodies and materials lost in other places said to appear in the lake, or the other way around—people have drowned in the lake and been found in other nearby bodies of water.

CURSE OF KASKASKIA. 1735, French girl falls for Indian.

They run away together, get captured, girl's father, Bernard, has Indian tied to a log and set adrift in the Mississippi. Before he dies, the Indian curses Bernard and the town. Bernard is killed in a duel the next year, the girl also dies. Over the next 200 years, the river cuts new channels, flooding Kaskaskia until everything is washed away, including churches and cemeteries. Devastating floods 1844, 1881, 1973. Many bodies lost to the river. Kaskaskia the first state capital of Illinois, now population of maybe a dozen.

SQUANDO'S CURSE, Saco River, Maine. Three whites a year

will die in the river because of the drowning of his son.

WISCONSIN LAKES CURSE. The last Indian who left Lake

Wingra (sometimes known as Dead Lake) said that the lake would die. Over the next fifty years, the lake shrunk dramatically, and as the <u>Wisconsin State Journal</u> noted in

1923, "has also become noted for its hidden whirlpools, and for its treachery." A Winnebago Indian was murdered on Maple Bluff overlooking Lake Mendota. He called upon the lake spirits to curse the white settlers, and kill two of them every year. From the same _Journal_ article: "Although this story is a fable, it is nevertheless true that scarcely a year has passed in the history of Madison, but that two whites have drowned in Mendota." Some fable.

CORNSTALK'S CURSE, Point Pleasant, West Virginia. Since Cornstalk's death in 1774, following disasters within 100 miles:

11/10/1777: Cornstalk killed, curses the land
1794: Point Pleasant incorporated
12/1907: Coal mine collapse kills 361, Monongah, WV
1913: Flood
4/1930: Prison fire in Columbus, OH, kills 320
1937: Flood
6/1944: Tornado kills 150
12/1967: Bridge collapse kills 46
8/1968: Plane crash kills 35
11/1970: Plane crash in Huntington, WV, kills 75
12/1972: 118 people killed in flood

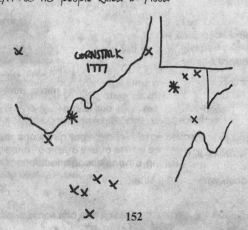

1/1978: Toxic spill contaminates city water supply
4/1978: 51 construction workers killed in power plant
   construction
Other coal-mine disasters: Eccles, Everettville, Osage,
Bartley, Benwood, Layland, Stuart

Mothman first seen in Point Pleasant. 100+ sightings in
the year before collapse of the Silver Bridge, centered in the
area about defunct West Virginia Ordnance Works. Rarely
seen after. Possible that later sightings were due to power
of suggestions, and Mothman was an omen figure? Whether
any of the 46 bridge collapse casualties saw the Mothman
is unknown.

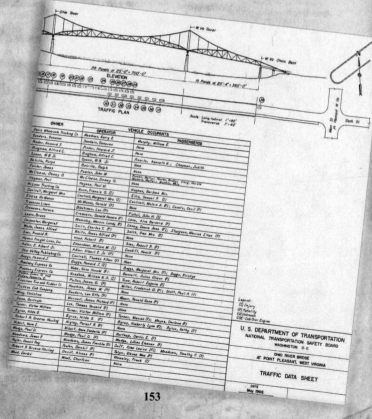

1998

January 24:

Dean's nineteenth. I was coming home from Vietnam right after my nineteenth. Dean's war isn't going to end like that. Had a dream last night that I found Mary's murderer, and knew that I would have to die to take him out. That's all right if it protects the boys.

Aum ("God's voice is Aum"), swastika (before Nazis, considered a good-luck symbol), ourobouros (derived from Milky Way, also Platonic idea of first living creature), Star of David (triangles chiral—Seal of Solomon?), ankh (hieroglyph "life")

April 17:

HOODOO ELEMENTS

Graveyard dirt: must leave an offering at the disturbed grave, coins or liquor. Mercury dime if possible—Mercury a psychopomp. Soldier's grave favored.

Goofer Dust: graveyard dirt, sulfur, salt. Anvil dust (power of blacksmith).

Four-leaf clover: from Celtic tradition that clover was a charm against evil spirits. First three leaves bring hope, faith, love. Fourth brings luck. Four-leaf clover also a quincunx.

Rattlesnake skin, rattle, or rattlesnake salt: chopped-up whole snake put in jar of salt, left for a period of time. Dried snake parts discarded, remaining salt has magical potency.

Coins: Mercury dime because of mythical associations. Mercury considered first metal in alchemy. Messenger god—ie, go-between, mediator. In voodoo, see Legba. Mercury also god of magicians, derived from Hermes. (Hermes Trimegistus, hermetic) Statues of Mercury and Hermes set at crossroads.

Fluids: blood, menstral fluid, urine, saliva, semen.

Hair: self if protective charm, intended focus if love or hex spell.

John the Conqueror root—form of morning glory, represents power of mythical African trickster sold into slavery.

Rabbit's foot: left hind especially. Rabbit should be taken in a cemetery if possible. Lucky because of association with hare as witches' familiar?

Conjure bag, mojo hand, nation sack. Color of fabric, contents of bag create different effects. Love, power, sex, luck.

Crossing marks: laid down in chalk, salt, crossroads dirt. Formula varies, but marks usually laid down in cross pattern—quincunx—with a circle around it. Wavy lines symbolically representing snakes also used. Patterns of small stones or marks made with the finger or a stick work when no crossing powder. Bad luck for the person the charm is intended for—sometimes also for whoever else crosses it.

Leftover elements should be discarded at a crossroads if possible.

May 2:

Sammy is fifteen today. He'll start high school this fall. Next spring he'll have a driver's license. Can't wait to have the boys fighting over the Impala. It's a little easier with Sammy lately. He seems more committed. Maybe that's because he's able to have more control over being in school, having a friend here and there. I try not to tell him what I really think, which is that he's shirking sometimes. Winchesters don't quit. I don't think he's quitting, but he gets stubborn, and then he won't listen to anything I say. He and Dean don't get along as well as they used to. Could be Sammy's getting tired of being the little brother, and always having Dean take the lead.

Could be it's time for Sammy to go out on his first solo. I should look around for something simple, like I did for Dean. Don't know why I'm so worried, really. Sammy's never hesitated when push came to shove.

May 5:

Sneeze on Monday, sneeze for danger. Sneeze on Tuesday, kiss a stranger. Sneeze on Wednesday, sneeze for a letter. Sneeze on Thursday, something better. Sneeze on Friday, sneeze for woe. Sneeze on Saturday, a journey to go. Sneeze on Sunday, your safety seek—for Satan will have you for the rest of the week!

Walking under ladders: from Egyptians. Leaned ladders on tomb walls so deceased could climb them, and spirits gathered in the triangle formed by the ladder, wall, and floor.

Chinese and Japanese heart-attack rates spike every month on the 4th. Superstition because words for "four" and "death" are homophones in both languages.

Knock on wood: from Druidic tradition of tapping on trees to ask resident spirits to come out.

Bulwer-Lytton
Conan Doyle
Yeats
Arthur Machen

May 17:

This would have been our twentieth anniversary. China. Mary and I never had china. We barely had Corningware. Twenty: four fives. Number of digits on the human body.

Hebrew/Arab: khamsa—"hand of Fatima" or "hand of Miriam." Arabic word means "five."
   Amulet, from Arabic hamala—"to carry"—related to Arabic tilasm, from Greek telesma or talein, where "talisman" comes from. Root has to do with initiation and mystery.
Contained gems, often turquoise in Arabic countries. Also contained everything else from hair to a baby's caul. Herbs, animal parts, coins, acorns, bamboo, bells, animal figurines, religious symbols, runes, crickets, drawings. Tattoos sometimes substituted. Turkish nazar.
   Marco Polo: "In an attempt of Kublai Khan to make a conquest of the island of Zipangu, a jealousy arose between the two commanders of the expedition, which led to an order for putting the whole garrison to the sword. In obedience to this order, the heads of all were cut off excepting of eight persons, who by the efficacy of a diabolical charm, consisting of a jewel or amulet introduced into the right arm, between the skin and the flesh, were

rendered secure from the effects of iron, either to kill or wound. Upon this discovery being made, they were beaten with a heavy wooden club, and presently died."

Amber prevents illness

Coral protects from evil

Opals increase magical strength

Sapphire is good fortune

Pearls for romance

Egyptian amulets: serapis protects against dangers from earth; canopus from water; a hawk from air; a snake from fire.

Levi: "The Pentagram must be always engraved on one side of the talisman, with a circle for the Sun, a crescent for the Moon, a winged caduceus for Mercury, a sword for Mars, a G for Venus, a crown for Jupiter, and a scythe for Saturn. The other side of the talisman should bear the sign of Solomon, that is, the six-pointed star formed by two interlaced triangles; in the centre there should be placed a human figure for the Sun talismans, a cup for those of the Moon, a dog's head for those of Jupiter, a lion's for those of Mars, a dove's for those of Venus, a bull's or goat's for those of Saturn. The names of the seven angels should be added either in Hebrew, Arabic, or magic characters similar to those of the alphabets of Trimethius. The two triangles of Solomon may be replaced by the double cross of Ezekiel's wheels, this being found on a great number of ancient pentacles. All objects of this nature, whether in metals or in precious stones, should be carefully

wrapped in silk satchels of a colour
analogous to the spirit of the planet,
perfumed with the perfumes of the
corresponding day, and preserved from
all impure looks and touches."

Seal of Solomon. Used to bind demons.

July 11:

The Fool, The Magician, The High Priestess, The Empress, The
Emperor, The Hierophant, The Lovers, The Chariot, Strength,
The Hermit, Wheel of Fortune, Justice, The Hanged Man,
Death, Temperance, The Devil, The Tower, The Star, The Moon,
The Sun, Judgment, The World.

Tarot as story. The Fool (whoever is asking for the
reading) must learn certain lessons. Order and connections
between the other cards tell the Fool's story.

August 4:

Back from Orlando with Sammy. Dean gave me some shuck
and jive about how he blazed through five states while we were
gone, but the Impala's odometer has barely budged. I'm guessing a girl is involved.

September 14:

Banshee. Bean sidhe. Sometimes they are dressed in white,
sometimes in a winding sheet or burial gown. They wail, they
scream, sometimes they sing to signal that death approaches
for some member of the household where they are heard.
Usually they come in one of three forms, which correspond
to the three stages of womanhood (and maybe have

something to do with the age of the person whose death is being signaled). A banshee is either a beautiful young woman, a matron, or a corpselike hag. As a hag, she has a link, way back, with notorious English hag figures such as Black Annis, a one-eyed crone, physically strong and with the features of a demon: long teeth, iron claws, and a blue face. She was said to hide in a giant oak that was the sole survivor of the primeval forest. Like many hag figures, she was a cannibal who preferred children, which she ate after flaying them alive. Their skins hung in a cave beneath the tree. (Link here to the Greek Lamia, a demonic/monstrous figure, often half-serpent, who eats children.)

Baba Yaga, from Russian lore, is another example. Living deep in the forest, in a magical hut that moved around on chicken legs, she often ate children, but unlike Black Annis, Baba Yaga could be an important source of magical help for a hero or questing child. If you asked her the right kind of question, or caught her in the right mood, she might help you on your errand instead of making a meal of you.

The banshee often appeared crying as she washed bloody clothes by a river—usually the clothes of someone about to die. Also, she can appear as a crow, rabbit, or weasel.

October 31:

Born on Halloween, said to convey gift of speaking to the dead

1424	Wladislaus III
1632	Jan Vermeer (possibly baptism)
1705	Clement XIV
1795	John Keats
1835	Adolf von Bayer
1887	Chiang Kai-Shek

1892   Alexander Alekhine
1896   Ethel Waters
1902   Abraham Wald
1912   Dale Evans
1918   Ian Stevenson
1922   Norodom Sihanouk
1930   Michael Collins
1931   Dan Rather
1950   Jane Pauley

Died on Halloween
1448   John VIII Palaeologus
1723   Cosimo de' Medici
1883   Swami Dayananda Saraswati
1926   Harry Houdini
1984   Indira Gandhi
1987   Joseph Campbell

Events
1517   Luther nails up 95 theses
1892   _Adventures of Sherlock Holmes_ published
1941   Mount Rushmore completed

Conan Doyle—_History of Spiritualism_, 1926. Eusapia
Palladino, Mina Crandon. Frauds.

November 2:

Mary has been dead for fifteen years. I feel like I'm getting
closer. Every year I learn a little more. Every supernatural
being I put away teaches me something. Every hunter I talk to
fills in another gap.

December 12:

Unsolved Serial Murders

1884-85	Austin, Texas—servant girls
1888	Jack the Ripper—probably springheel
1918-19	Axeman of New Orleans—claimed to be a demon, in letters
1935-38	Cleveland Torso killer (possibly active 20s-50s)
1946	Texarkana, Phantom Killer
1968-84	Capital City murders, Madison, WI
1968-69	Zodiac killer, California—possibly active 1963-71
1971-76	Alphabet killer, upstate NY
1975-90	Area of New Haven, CT—young women
1976-77	Oakland County, MI. Child killer
1976-86	Coastal California—linked to East Area Rapist in Oakland?
1979-86	Night Stalker, California
1980s	Southside Slayer, Los Angeles
1982-	Green River Killer

Ciudad Juarez—hundreds(?) of young women

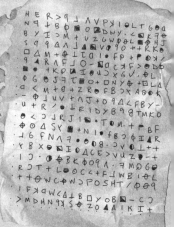

December 28:

Howling of dogs a death omen. From Egyptians? Jackal-headed Anubis conducted souls to the afterlife. Mesoamerican and Native American, also African belief that dogs led spirits to the underworld. Persians kept dogs by their deathbeds to ward off evil spirits that might prey on departed souls.

1999

January 1:

Figured I would try to put together a sort of Revenant 101. The lore is all over the place, so probably some experimenting is needed to settle on best tactics. The European sources say revenants, including vampires, may be destroyed by:

Staking. Ash or oak most effective. Rom traditions use hawthorn. Generally stakes are driven into the heart, but sometimes the mouth or stomach. Wooden stakes employed sometimes to destroy the revenant, sometimes to pin it in the coffin. Corpse can be staked through the legs to keep it from getting out. Variation on staking: use metal pins or needles—piercing heart, eyes, or feet. Sharp metal objects buried with corpse keep it in place, often a sickle. Pieces of steel or iron placed in the mouth.

Burning. Corpse suspected of being a dormant revenant exhumed and burned. Sometimes only the heart must be burned. Some traditions burn the body and mix the ashes with water or holy water. Surviving relatives drink the mixture, releasing the curse.

Dismembered or decapitated. Heart cut out, or head severed and placed between the feet. Head sometimes buried in a separate location, or burned. 1892, Mercy Brown, Rhode Island. Father thought she was a vampire, dug her up, burned her heart.

Exorcism. Performed when the body is believed to be possessed instead of revenant.

New World vampires: tunda, soucouyant, patasola, peuchen, cihuateteo (sunlight fatal), asema (becomes ball of light like African obayifo), lobishomen (unleashes women's sexual drive)

Asia: jiangshi, bhuta, prēt, bramarakshasa, mandurugo/penanggalan (succubus qualities), pontianak/langsuir (died in childbirth like Aztec mocihuaquetzqui), leyak, aswang, manananggal (preys on pregnant women), nukekubi, chural (feet backwards like leszy?), kappa (lives in water, noted for etiquette but drains life force)

Africa: ramanga, adze (changes into firefly), asasabosam, impundulu

Europe: callicantzaros (born between Christmas and Epiphany, can only attack on those days), upis (two hearts), ustrel (born on Saturday, died unbaptized)

Australia: yama-yha-who. Victims gradually transformed into the creature by its feeding on them, or if it ate them whole and then vomited them back up

Akhanavar, Armenian vampire that drains blood through the feet

January 24:

Dean turns twenty today. He's in Ohio somewhere, hasn't called in a couple of days. Tracking a possible poltergeist. He's supposed to call in every night. Mission discipline is critical.

March 21:

Dighton Rock, Massachusetts. Saw it yesterday. Looks like prehistoric version of bathroom graffiti to me, but some of the symbols must mean something. Indian? Viking? Theories about Portuguese explorer Miguel Cortereal, 1511?

Other megaliths in New England. The Vikings were here, everyone knows it. What might they have brought? What might they have left behind? Their runes can't all be hoaxes, and Viking runes were divine, Odin earned them by hanging on his tree.

May 2:

Corpus Hermeticum, *"The Secret Sermon on the Mountain."*

Torment the first is this Not-knowing, son; the second one is Grief; the third, Intemperance; the fourth, Concupiscence; the fifth, Unrighteousness; the sixth is Avarice; the seventh, Error; the eighth is Envy; the ninth, Guile; the tenth is Anger; eleventh, Rashness; the twelfth is Malice. These are in number twelve; but under them are many more, my son; and creeping through the prison of the body they force the man that's placed therein to suffer in his senses.

Sammy is sixteen years old today. God knows he's got plenty of torments. Now he's got a driver's license, too. Doesn't make much difference. He's known how to drive since he was nine.

May 17:

This would have been our twenty-first anniversary. Mary, I've been doing this for almost sixteen years, and sometimes I feel like I'm not any closer to an answer than I was when I watched the house burn in 1983. What am I doing? I've thrown everything away for this, to join an underground tribe of hunters and spend my nights watching exorcisms and killing spirits . . . and what have I done to the boys? They don't have friends, not the way I did. I lived in the same town the whole time I was growing up. Now they're almost grown, and they've seen every back road and abandoned farmhouse in the country, but they don't have roots. We've never been back to Lawrence.

Wonder how many exorcisms I've seen. Maybe fifty, sixty? How many of them were real demons, and how many were some other kind of prankster spirit? Anything can call itself a demon. I've smelled the sulfur, though. I've seen the holy water and the Devil's Traps work. The whole thing might be easier if the demons weren't so cagey about the Big Guy down there. If they've never seen him, and most of them don't believe he exists, then hey, there's no fallen angels ruling over Hell. So no angels, period. And then what are demons? And what is Hell? They (creatures that say they're demons) say it exists.

21: three 7s. The Fool must learn 21 lessons in the Tarot story.

Sixth book of Moses. Seals.

November 2:

Mary has been dead for sixteen years. The century's ending, by popular reckoning. Wonder what's waiting on the other side.

Dybbuk. A malicious possessing spirit/soul of someone recently dead. Escaped from or prevented entry into the afterlife (especially in the case of suicide). Derived from the Hebrew word meaning "attachment"—dybbuk possesses a living person, usually to finish a task that it was prevented from performing in life. Drawn to people who have unfulfilled desires to do something, possibly something unethical or wrong is more attractive to the spirit. Possession makes the person more likely to do the things he's been preventing himself from doing, and dybbuk can be drawn to a person who wants the same things it wanted in life. If the dybbuk is allowed to finish, or helped along its way, it will depart when the goal is accomplished. Dybbuks described in Samuel 18:10 and Book of Kings when Elijah is possessed by a spirit trying to get Saul to start an unjust war.

Jewish exorcism involving Psalm 91 and the blowing of a ram's horn to shatter the walls surrounding the dybbuk.

1 He that dwelleth in the secret place of the Most High shall abide under the shadow of the Almighty.

2 I will say of the LORD, He is my refuge and my fortress: my God; in Him will I trust.

3 Surely He shall deliver thee from the snare of the fowler, and from the noisome pestilence.

4 He shall cover thee with His feathers, and under His wings shalt thou trust: His truth shall be thy shield and buckler.

5 Thou shalt not be afraid for the terror by night; nor for the arrow that flieth by day;

6 nor for the pestilence that walketh in darkness; nor for the destruction that wasteth at noonday.

7 A thousand shall fall at thy side, and ten thousand at thy right hand; but it shall not come nigh thee.

8 Only with thine eyes shalt thou behold and see the reward of the wicked.

9 Because thou hast made the LORD, which is my refuge, even the Most High, thy habitation;

10 there shall no evil befall thee, neither shall any plague come nigh thy dwelling.

11 For He shall give his angels charge over thee, to keep thee in all thy ways.

12 They shall bear thee up in their hands, lest thou dash thy foot against a stone.

13 Thou shalt tread upon the lion and adder: the young lion and the dragon shalt thou trample under feet.

14 Because He hath set His love upon me, therefore will I deliver Him: I will set Him on high, because He hath known my name.

15 He shall call upon me, and I will answer Him: I will be with Him in trouble; I will deliver Him, and honor Him.

16 With long life will I satisfy Him, and show Him my salvation.

Commentaries on the psalm emphasize the safety of the righteous man in the face of surprise dangers. Hebrew commentaries suggest that pestilence and destruction are poetic names for demons, one coming by night and the other at noon.

Jinn. From Semitic root meaning hidden. Pre-Islamic Arabian myth said they were the spirits of vanished peoples who brought disease and insanity at night. Also said to be spirits of fire who could change shape. Advent of Islam changed their character. Koran says they were created of smokeless fire. Particular varieties may or may not be identified with ordinal directions or elements; ifrit, marid, etc. All can be bound through ritual or if they can be overpowered. In hadith, elements of shape-changing remain, and an ifrit attacks Muhammad with a firebolt.

Koran, sura 72, al-Jinn:

Say (O Muhammad): It is revealed unto me that a company of the Jinn gave ear, and they said: Lo! we have heard a marvellous Koran, which guideth unto righteousness, so we believe in it and we ascribe no partner unto our Lord. And (we believe) that He—exalted be the glory of our Lord!—hath taken neither wife nor son, And that the foolish one among us used to speak concerning Allah an atrocious lie. And lo! we had supposed that humankind and jinn would not speak a lie concerning Allah—and indeed (O Muhammad) individuals of humankind used to invoke the protection of individuals of the jinn, so that they increased them in revolt against Allah; And indeed they supposed, even as ye suppose, that Allah would not raise anyone (from the dead). And (the Jinn who had listened to the Koran said): We had sought the heaven but had found it filled with strong warders and meteors. And we used to sit on places (high) therein to listen. But he who listeneth now findeth a flame in wait for him; and we know not whether harm is boded unto all who are in the earth, or whether their Lord intendeth guidance for them. And among us there are righteous folk and among us there are far from that. We are sects having different rules. And we know that we cannot escape from Allah in the earth, nor can we escape by flight. And when we heard the guidance, we believed therein, and whoso believeth in his Lord, he feareth neither loss nor oppression. And there are among us some who have surrendered (to Allah) and there are among us some who are unjust. And whoso hath surrendered to Allah, such have taken the right path purposefully. And as for those who are unjust, they are firewood for hell.

The Letters, or Characters of Saturne.

The Letters, or Characters of Jupiter.

The Letters, or Characters of Mars.

The Letters, or Characters of the Sun.

The Letters, or Characters of Venus.

The Letters, or Characters of Mercury.

The Letters, or Characters of the Moon.

2000

January 1:

Y2K didn't end the world. New Year's Eve almost did Dean in, though. He's upstairs, immobile. I don't feel good myself.

January 17:

1/5   Telsphorus
1/11 Hyginus
1/14 Felix of Nola
1/16 Marcellus I
1/18 Prisca—lion wouldn't eat her
1/19 Marius, Martha, Audifax, Abachumm; Canute—Danish king killed by peasants
1/20 Fabian, Sebastian
1/21 Agnes—beheaded after fire wouldn't burn
1/22 Vincent, Anastasius
1/23 Emerentiana—Agnes's nurse
1/24 Timothy—stoned by pagans
1/26 Polycarp—tutor of Irenaeus
1/30 Martina

2/1   Ignatius—died in arena
2/3   Blase
2/5   Agatha

2/6   Dorothy
2/9   Apollonia—teeth pulled
2/14 Valentine
2/15 Faustinus, Jovita
2/18 Simeon—crucified

3/4   Lucius I
3/6   Perpetua and Felicity
3/10 Forty Holy Martyrs—frozen to death

4/13 Hermenegild
4/14 Tiburtius, Valerian, Maximus
4/17 Anicetus
4/22 Soter and Cajus
4/23 George
4/24 Fidelis of Sigmaringen
4/26 Cletus, Marcellinus
4/29 Peter—assassinated by Cathars

5/3 Alexander I, Eventius, Theodulus
5/7 Stanislaus—killed by King Boleslaw
5/12 Nereus, Achilleus, Domitilla, Pancras
5/14 Boniface
5/18 Venantius
5/25 Urban I
5/26 Eleutherius
5/27 John I
5/30 Felix I

6/2 Marcellinus, Peter, Erasmus
6/5 Boniface
6/9 Primus and Felician
6/12 Basilides, Cyrinus, Nabor, Nazarius
6/15 Vitus, Modestus, and Crescentia
6/18 Mark and Marcellianus
6/19 Gervase and Protase
6/20 Silverius
6/26 John and Paul

7/2 Processus and Martinian
7/3 Irenaeus
7/10 Rufina, Secunda
7/11 Pius I
7/12 Nabor and Felix
7/18 Symphorosa and her seven sons—watched her sons killed
7/20 Margaret
7/23 Apollinaris
7/24 Christina
7/27 Pantaleon
7/28 Nazarius, Celsus, Victor I
7/29 Felix II, Simplicius, Faustinus, Beatrice
7/30 Abdon, Sennen

8/1 Holy Machabees
8/2 Stephen I
8/6 Xystus II, Felicissimus, and Agapitus
8/8 Cyriacus, Largus, and Smaragdus
8/9 Romanus
8/10 Laurence
8/11 Tiburtius and Susanna—walked on hot coals
8/13 Hippolytus and Cassian
8/18 Agapitus
8/22 Timothy and companions
8/26 Zephyrinus
8/28 Hermes
8/29 John the Baptist, Sabina
8/30 Felix and Adauctus

9/1 Holy Twelve Brothers
9/8 Hadrian—limbs cut off on an anvil, lightning killed executioners
9/9 Gorgonius
9/11 Protus and Hyacinth
9/15 Nicomedes
9/16 Cornelius, Cyprian, Euphemia, Lucy, and Geminianus
9/19 Januarius and companions
9/20 Eustace and companions
9/22 Maurice and companions
9/23 Linus, Thecla
9/26 Cyprian and Justina
9/27 Cosmas and Damian
9/28 Wenceslaus

10/5 Placid and companions
10/8 Sergius, Bacchus, Marcellus, and Apuleius
10/9 Eleutherius

10/14 Callistus I
10/21 Ursula and companions
10/25 Chrysanthus and Daria—
buried alive
10/26 Evaristus

11/4 Vitalis and Agricola—Vitalis in
arena, Agricola crucified
11/8 Holy Four Crowned Martyrs
11/9 Theodore
11/10 Tryphon, Respicius, and
Nympha
11/11 Mennas
11/12 Martin I
11/14 Josaphat
11/19 Pontianus

11/22 Cecilia
11/23 Clement I, Felicitas
11/24 Chrysogonus
11/25 Catherine
11/26 Peter of Alexandria

12/2 Bibiana
12/4 Barbara
12/10 Melchiades
12/13 Lucy
12/16 Eusebius
12/25 Anastasia
12/26 Stephen Protomartyr
12/28 Holy Innocents
12/29 Thomas

Plants and herbs used in contacting dark spirits: acacia, devil pod, mullein, valerian.

Eucalyptus, salt, garlic, rosemary, bay leaves for protection.

Mint, hyssop, rue, sage, yarrow for breaking spells or malign influence.

January 24:

Dean turns twenty-one today. I'd buy him a beer if I thought it would be something new. He's also old enough to buy his own guns now. I tried to raise him right, and looks like I did. He's a scam artist, a ladies' man, and an absolutely loyal son. He knows what's right and doesn't hesitate to do it. I'm proud of him. Now that he's hunting on his own I don't see as much of him, but I know he's out there. When I call him in on a job, he's right there every time. I've spent the last sixteen years afraid that I was going to screw him up somehow. Maybe now I can forget about that.

February 5:

NON TIMEBO MALA—inscribed on Colt? "I will fear no evil."

Agrippa: "The manner of making these kinds of Magical Rings is this, viz.: When any Star ascends fortunately, with the fortunate aspect or conjunction of the Moon, we must take a stone and herb that is under that Star, and make a ring of the metal that is suitable to this Star, and in it fasten the stone, putting the herb or root under it—not omitting the inscriptions of images, names, and characters . . ."

So what star was the Colt made under? If it's iron, must be Mars. Tuesday. October 27, November 5, November 12. Davy Crockett leaves for Texas on November 1.

February 28:

Agrimony: protection, reversal. As infusion, sleep
Amaranth: dried flowers used in calling spirits, necromancy
Angelica: apotropaic, good luck
Asafetida: used in exorcisms, attracts wolves
Basil: used in exorcisms
Bay: visions, prophetic dreams
Belladonna: funerary rites, passage of souls
Betony: purifies
Bindweed: control
Buchu: divination
Carob: burned to repel poltergeists
Clove: exorcism, purification
Cubeb: repel demons
Devil's bit: intensifier, control
Fennel: repels evil, unpredictable
Frankincense: exorcism, protection, divination, balance

Garlic: sacrificed to Hecate at crossroads. Protective, courage

Horehound: protection during exorcism

Mandrake: powerful because of humanoid shape. Homunculi made from it. Whole root protective in demonology

Mistletoe: exorcism, protection

Mugwort: divination, summoning

St. John's Wort: repels demons, evil spirits

Willow: protection, divination

Yarrow: divination

April 30:

REVENANTS

GHOUL. From Arabian/Persian legends, dwells in graveyards or uninhabited places. Ghul literally means demon, but the ghoul doesn't behave in the way Judeo-Christian demons do. Sired by Iblis (primary devil of Islam, a jinn who rebelled against Allah and was allowed to roam the earth to test people by putting bad ideas in their heads). Also the name for a desert-dwelling shape-shifting demon, often seen as a hyena. Lures travelers into the desert to eat them, also kidnaps children. Ghouls rob and desecrate graves, eat the dead.

VETALA. Vampiric spirit from Hindu myth which animates corpses, haunts cemeteries, causes miscarriages. Can tell the future and reveal hidden secrets if captured. Destroyed by the performing of a proper funeral.

DRAUGR. Icelandic/Viking legend, undead beings who are enormously strong and can grow or shrink in size. Escaped the grave by turning into smoke. Unclear whether any of the dead person's personality survived in the draugr. Draugr can't be hurt by regular weapons, must be wrestled back into their graves. Final disposal methods recall vampire-killing instructions: decapitate, burn, and scatter the ashes in the sea. Some draugr (haugbui) stayed at their graves. Others sometimes marauded through settlements. Related to the draug, a Nordic sea-ghost and death omen. Spirit—sometimes corporeal—of drowned sailor. One variant, the gleip, causes bad luck—makes sailors slip on wet rocks. Draug can also change their appearance to look like stones.

Sometimes in this form they are taken aboard ships as ballast, and when they reassume their natural form they capsize the ship. As death omen, draug are said to scream like banshee, and sometimes they are only seen by the man who is about to die.

Also from Scandinavia, the myling or utburd (meaning something cast out). Spirits or incarnations of children who died before being baptized, or were murdered. Leap on the backs of travelers at night, wanting to be buried in hallowed ground. Myling grows heavier the closer it gets to the graveyard, eventually pressing its carrier down into the earth. Myling kills those who cannot complete this task.

May 2:

Sammy is seventeen years old today. I'm going to guess that he's the only sophomore in the United States who has read the *Clavicula Solomonis* and made parts of it work. Bought him a new computer. He's a zealot about having a Macintosh. Also he's a walking dictionary of the occult and esoteric. There's a lot of his mother in Sammy. God, I wish he had some way to know that other than me telling him.

May 15:

Barrett on a spirit book: This book being thus perfected, let it be brought, in a clear and fair night, to a circle prepared in a cross-way, according to the art which we have before delivered; and there, in the first place, the book is to be opened, and to be consecrated according to the rites and ways which we have before delivered concerning consecration, which being done, let all the spirits be called which are written in the book, in their own order and place, conjuring them thrice by the bonds described in the book that they come to that place within the space of three days, to assure their obedience and confirm the same, to the book so to be consecrated; then let the book be wrapped up in a clean linen cloth, and bury it in the midst of the circle, and stop the hole so as it may not be perceived or discovered: the circle being destroyed after you have licensed the spirits, depart before sun-rise; and on the third day, about the middle of the night, return and make the circle anew and on thy knees make prayer unto God, and give thanks to him; and let a precious perfume be made, open the hole in which you buried your book and take it out, and so let it be kept, not opening the same. Then after licensing the spirits in their order and destroying the circle, depart before sunrise.

To be written in the double circle around a pentacle:

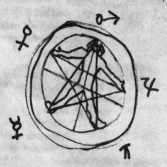

   Ten general names—El, Elohim, Elohe, Zebaoth, Elion, Escerchie, Adonay, Jah, Tetragrammaton, Saday—together with versicle appropriate to the nature of the conjuration.
   Astrological signs of planets desired to strengthen the summoning or binding.

May 17:

This would have been our twenty-second anniversary. Every year, the more I learn about communicating with the dead, the harder it gets not to talk to you, Mary. I dream about it, I stop myself at least once a week from digging out a ritual and bringing you to me, even if it's only for a few minutes. Then what happened with Jim stops me. I don't think I could stand to see that happen again. You're alive to me because I think of nothing but avenging you. That's the way it has to be.

June 3:

   Pyromancy—fire
   Aeromancy—air, wind
   Aquamancy—language of running water
   Cartomancy—tarot

Haruspication—entrails
Augury—birdsong
Oneiromancy—dreams

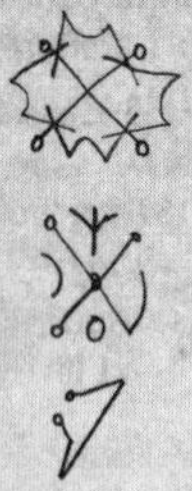

John Gaule's _Mysmantia_, 1652, mentions others:
Alphitomancy—flour, meal
Antinopomancy—entrails of women and children
Arithmancy—numbers
Astragalomancy—dice
Astromancy—stars and planets
Axinomancy—saws
Botanomancy—herbs
Captromancy—smoke
Carromancy—melting wax
Catoxtromancy—mirrors
Cephalonomancy—broiling an ass's head
Chiromancy—hands
Crystallomancy—glasses
Coscinomancy—sieves
Dactylomancy—rings
Gastronomancy—sounds from the belly
Geomancy—earth
Gyromancy—circles
Lampadomancy—candles and lamps
Lithomancy—stones
Livanomancy—burning of frankincense
Logarithmancy—logarithms
Macharomancy—knives or swords
Oenomancy—wine
Omphilomancy—navel
Onomatomancy—names
Onychomancy—fingernails
Podomancy—feet

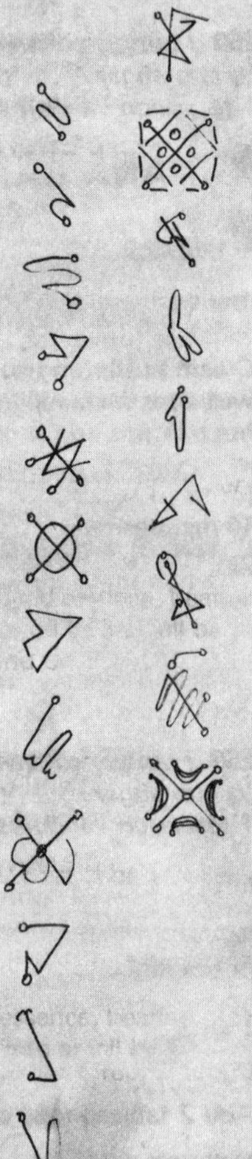

Roadomancy—stars
Sciomancy—shadows
Spatalamancy—offal
Sycomancy—figs
Tuphramancy—ashes
Tyromancy—ashes

SNEEDS LINER—ETRUSCAN

September 15:

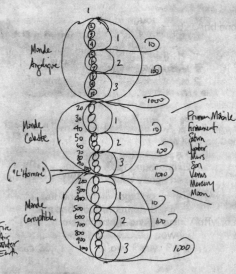

Monde Angélique

Monde Céleste

("L'Homme")

Monde Corruptible

Fire
Air
Water
Earth

Primum Mobile
Firmament
Saturn
Jupiter
Mars
Sun
Venus
Mercury
Moon

PICO DELLA MIRANDOLA

TORNADO   SUNDOWNER
HURRICANE   SQUAMISH
JETSTREAM   CHINOOK
DUST DEVIL   DIABLO
MATANUSKA   KNIK
SANTA ANA   TAKU

October 11:

EVP: Can record voices of the dead, sometimes
unintentionally. Not always intended as communication.
Sometimes it's more like eavesdropping. Worth a shot in most
hauntings, from what I hear. Either you get nothing, so you
lose nothing, or you hear something that helps identify the
spirit. Spooky collection of recordings at the roadhouse, but it's
been, what . . . ten years since we were there?

November 2:

Mary has been dead for seventeen years. She's watching. Time doesn't pass in heaven.

Or in Hell?

December 8:

Names for Hell/afterlife: Hamistagan. Aaru. Elysium, Hades, Tartarus. Valhalla, Hel, Niflheim. Sheol, Olam Haba, Gehenna, Shamayim, Raquia, Shehaqim, Machonon, Machon, Zebul, Araboth. Jannah, Firdaws, Pardis, Jahannam, Jahim, Zamharir, Hutamah, Ladza, Saqor. Bardo. Mictlan, Tlalocan. Naraka, Swarga Loka. Diyu, Tian. Duat. Yomi. Xibalba, Metnal. Adilvun, Shobari Waka. Gimokodan, Kalichi. Hetgwauge. Aralu. Anaon. Uffern. Manala.

Monikers and nicknames for Satan: Father of Lies, Prince of Darkness, Old Nick, Old Scratch, Beelzebub, Mephistopheles, the Adversary, Old Harry, the Old Gentleman, Lucifer, Diabolos, Rex Mundi

Tritone, augmented fourth, known as "the devil in musick" from early medieval times. Composers stayed away from it in sacred music. Now every half-baked metal band is in love with it.

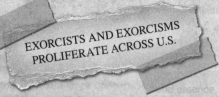

EXORCISTS AND EXORCISMS
PROLIFERATE ACROSS U.S.

NY archdiocese investigates 40+ per year
Improvised exorcisms kill victims

2001

January 24:

Happy 22, Dean. Hope you're enjoying Arkansas.

March 18:

Clown Jester Memento Mori. Trickster? Loki. Coyote, Raven,
Heyoka, Nanabozho, Azeban, Mannegishi, Wisakedjak, Amaguq.
Sosruko. Puck, Eshu, Anansi. Bamapana. Sun Wukong. Reynard,
Till Eulenspiegel. Brer Rabbit, Bugs Bunny.

   Not always fun and games. Trickster levels, brings the
high low and gives the low a laugh. Tricks can be deadly
because the trickster operates outside codified social norms,
so is not bound by taboos. Can switch gender, change shape,
sow chaos. Related back to clowns in Ute stories of siats,
clown monsters who eat children. Female version, bapet,
suckled with poisonous milk. Eastern version is Hagondes.

   Fearsome Critters—lumber folklore. Albotritch, Argopelter,
Augerino, Axhandle Hound, Ball-tailed Cat, Bed Cat, Billdad,
Cactus Cat, Camp Chipmunk, Central American Whintosser,
Clubtailed Glyptodont, Columbia River Sand Squink, Come-at-
a-Body, Cougar-Fish, Cuba, Dew-Mink, Ding Ball, Dismal Sauger,
Dungaven-Hooter, Flibbertigibbet, Flitterick, Funeral Mountain
Terrashot, Gazerium, Giddy Fish, Glawackus, Goofang,
Goofus Bird, Gumberoo, Guyascutus, Hang-down, Happy Auger,

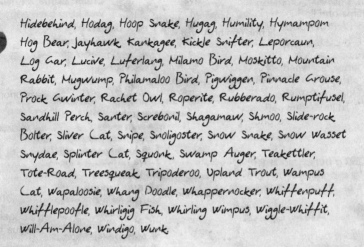

Hidebehind, Hodag, Hoop Snake, Hugag, Humility, Hymampom Hog Bear, Jayhawk, Kankagee, Kickle Snifter, Leporcaun, Log Gar, Lucive, Luferlang, Milamo Bird, Moskitto, Mountain Rabbit, Mugwump, Philamaloo Bird, Pigwiggen, Pinnacle Grouse, Prock Gwinter, Rachet Owl, Roperite, Rubberado, Rumptifusel, Sandhill Perch, Santer, Screbonil, Shagamaw, Shmoo, Slide-rock Bolter, Sliver Cat, Snipe, Snoligoster, Snow Snake, Snow Wasset Snydae, Splinter Cat, Squonk, Swamp Auger, Teakettler, Tote-Road, Treesqueak Tripoderoo, Upland Trout, Wampus Cat, Wapaloosie, Whang Doodle, Whappernocker, Whiffenpuff, Whifflepoofle, Whirligig Fish, Whirling Wimpus, Wiggle-Whiffit, Will-Am-Alone, Windigo, Wunk.

Hoop-snake: ourobouros
Wendigo
Flibbertigibbet: applied to witches, name of a demon in King Lear, possibly another name for Puck

May 2:

Sammy is eighteen years old today. Surprised he didn't take off. We're not getting along too well. He hunts when we need him to, but he's never committed himself the way Dean did. Dean's never known any other way to live, or if he has, he doesn't act like it. He's playing the role he was born to play. Sammy's the younger brother. He doesn't know what his role is, even though I can tell him until I'm blue in the face and we're both ready to kill each other. He's got one more year of school and then I'm drafting him full-time into the family business. I've given him more slack than I ever gave Dean, more than I would have ever gotten from my dad. He needed it. Now he's a grown man, or almost. Time for him to step into what's expected of him. Dean never even thought about college. We used to joke about it once in a while. But Sammy still believes he can have a normal life, but they're both more useful to the world as hunters than . . . what, lawyers? Dentists? Sammy's convinced himself that smart kids have to go to college. Part of my job is to convince him that college would be a waste of his smarts. And I gotta hand it to him on the brains front: there's nothing he can't find on the computer. I still dig around in actual books, libraries, newspapers. It's all keystrokes and search words for Sammy. He's done a good job hiding our trail on all the credit cards.

May 4:

2510 23rd, Boulder CO	40° 01' N 105° 17' W
1223 Sherman, Ypsilanti MI	42° 14' N 83° 37' W
21 Harmon, Portland ME	43° 39' N 70° 16' W
505 E. 20th, New York	40° 43' N 74° 00' W

La Cueva, near Mesilla NM. Hermit with healing powers lived in this cave. Was murdered, and found on a crucifix wearing a girdle of spikes. Murder unsolved, but hermit's ghost said to appear on Friday nights at sundown.

May 17:

This would have been our twenty-third anniversary. Now the new century is really here, and I'm still on the hunt. Getting closer? Bobby threw me this curveball the other day:

Admitting that demons exist might not be the same as believing in demons—esp. since the demons don't even believe. Even if they aren't demons, if they think they are—if they're some kind of spirit that believes itself a demon—then they're going to act like demons are supposed to act.

In other words, even if demons aren't real, as long as there are malevolent spirits that think they're demons and act like demons, they'll need to be fought like demons. Kind of a spin on the thoughtform, created from belief . . . ?

Sounds too complicated to me. Either there are demons or there aren't.

Another Seal of Solomon:

June 20:

John Dee. 1527-1608. Chose coronation date of Queen Elizabeth, signed his letters to her with 007. Knew Mercator, Tycho Brahe. Propaedeumata Aphoristica, 1558. Quinti Libri Mysteriorum. Monas Hierglyphica, 1564. Enochian language and alphabet. Tried to syncretize Hermetic, Pythagorean, Christian traditions, Kabbalistic belief that numbers were the basis of reality and understanding. Gravestone disappeared after his death.

July 18:

Enoch one of the Judeo-Christian tradition's crazy magnets. Supposedly taken up into heaven at the age of 365, transformed into the angel Metatron. In Islamic tradition, Idris. Pre-Judaic Watchers tales have Enoch as one of the angels who taught men the first sciences, and how things worked. In variant stories, Enoch is a giant—son of the fallen angels? Nephilim? Great-grandfather of Noah. Brought writing and arts, therefore considered a father of language. Dee picks up on this, tries to recover original Enochian language.

You have to be soft-headed to believe in angels. But I've written down every random esoteric thing I've run across, just in case it might be a clue. Someone who didn't know me before reading this journal would think I was crazy.

September 11:

Shaken. 11 is the number of sin, between the perfection of 10—digits on the fingers—and the holiness of 12—Zodiac signs, apostles, hours of day and night . . . I can't believe that a handful of religious nuts with boxcutters could do something like this. There must be more to it. Have been on the phone with every hunter I know today, and it's unanimous. Everyone's talking demons, nobody has any details but nobody thinks that what's on the surface is all there is. I'm going to New York to look around. Meeting a couple of other guys there.

Tuesday. Mars.

Feast of Protus and Hyacinth. Martyred by Valerian, burned. Valerian used in rituals to contact angry spirits, demons. Something here that I'm not putting together.

September 15:

God, the spirits in Shanksville. The story coming out is bull.

Looking for sigils that resemble any of these.

November 2:

Eighteen years.

December 19:

Boyd Sanatorium, New Mexico. Built to treat his wife, then Boyd became deranged, subjected patients to experimental treatments. Place is neck-deep in spirits.

INVENTORY
Curse box—rabbit's foot
Letter from Samuel Colt to gunsmith
Bag of alligator teeth
Too damn many books
Jar, dead homunculus
Papers
Colt Peacemaker, inscribed barrel
Cassettes with EVP from Skokie, Brooklyn, Paw Paw,
Dalhart, Elko—Gary has the rest
All kinds of other crap
Abrasax ring, bronze, Greek inscription around inside
Jar of dirt from Devil's Gate
Slug mold, 56 oz pure silver
Dozen or so mojo hands

2002

January 24:

Dean turns twenty-three today. It's a good age, twenty-three. You're starting not to be a kid anymore, and you're still young enough that you feel invincible physically. Forty-eight doesn't feel like that at all.

February 2:

Demon's Alley, West Milford NJ. Entire neighborhood of abandoned houses. Stories of cult massacre, ritual sacrifice. Unable to substantiate.

March 3:

Leonardo NJ. Dempsey house. Murder/suicide, bodies burned in basement boilers. Haunted by policeman who killed family, also his wife and children. The rope was hard to burn.

March 8:

Sam told me and Dean today that he is going to Stanford. I told him that if he goes, he better stay gone. I think Dean would have taken a swing at him if I hadn't kept my cool. Barely. Trying to work out what to do about this. We can't tolerate any of us quitting. We're better as a team. I've protected Sammy his whole life, and so has Dean. Could be I've gone too easy on him. Dean always responded to discipline because he believed in the mission. I thought that by giving Sammy more room, I'd let him find his own way to dedication like Dean's. Doesn't look like that worked out. Now he's a straight-A student, computer whiz . . . I think he's gone a little soft. How many tight spots have we been in since he was a baby? And now he's going to college? He can go to hell, is where he can go.

March 29:

Got a call from Missouri. Stull Church was torn down last night by persons unknown. The building was rickety as hell, but still I can't help wonder if it's related somehow . . . but if it is, why now? There's nothing about the date, nothing else going on in the area that I've heard about. Its spirits will still be there, though. They don't care about the building. Whatever goes up in the church's place is going to have bad atmosphere. Wonder if the foundation was torn out, and what might be in there.

April 10:

Daeva: Zoroastrian creatures/ demons. Once characterized as false gods, later demons of chaos and disorder. More recently believed to be incarnations of pure evil. Younger Avesta opposes them to the gods of light. Named daevas: Angra Mainyu (later Ahriman), Sarva, Indra, Nanghaithya, Tauru, Zairi, Nasu. Also another demon, Paitisha. Daevas vulnerable to fire, and drawn to the physical processes of the human body. Also they are attracted by speaking during meals. Tradition in medieval Zoroastrianism discouraged eating after dark since daevas were out then. Book of Arda Wiraz *describes them spreading across the Earth at nightfall, causing destruction—both personal and on a larger scale. Daevas sometimes blamed for natural disasters that happened at night. Occasionally they are given incubus-like properties. About three dozen daevas named in Zian texts, and more referred to.*

May 2:

Sammy is nineteen today. He's got some decisions to make.

May 17:

This would have been our twenty-fourth anniversary. Funny how after twenty years, there's a five- or ten-year gap between special gift years. What would I have given you, Mary? A clock, for 24 hours in the day? A Tanakh, which has 24 books? A piece of 24-karat pure gold jewelry? Gold doesn't come until 50 years, though. Getting a little too drunk to keep coming up with ideas.

June 13:

Sam graduated. He didn't go to the ceremony. I think he's still carrying a grudge that it took him an extra year. What do you want me to do, Sammy? Should we have stayed in Lawrence while whatever killed your mother came back for you? Should we have sat around fat, dumb, and happy even though war had been declared? How long would we have lasted that way?

July 30:

Now in Hibbing County, Minnesota—this county has more missing persons per capita than anywhere in the state. Very few of these cases have been solved. There are people here who speak of a "phantom attacker." Is Hibbing a possible hunting ground? Why are there so many missing from here? Some of these date back generations. I have spoken to a few of the locals, there are rumors about a dark figure who comes out at night, takes a victim, and vanishes. No trace of victims. Some people hear unusual sounds close to the place the victims have disappeared. Is this just a local legend or some kind of phantom? (Like Springheel Jack, phantom gassers, etc.?)

Known Missing Persons. History.

Date	Name
1899	Jay Robins / Mike McCarthy
1899	Campbell Watson / Randy Holden
1900	Jonathan Ducette / Avo Liva
1900	Ross Framo / Ed Daniels
Lost period records ———— fire.	
1985	Tom Chen / Lawrence Lau
1986	Chris Thompson / John Crockett
1987	George Nidas / Ruth Elkie
1988	JoJo MacDowall / Maria Waterman
1989	Bren Moore / Unknown victim
1990	Kelly Bruhm / Brenda Knight
1991	Joanne Riley / Norm Collins
1992	Harvey Fedor / Charlie Schultz
1993	Dave Riopel / Gizelle Fredette
1994	Paul Thompson / Tracey Tyerman
1995	Milhan Dance / David Neveux
1996	Tony Beck / Don Tupper
1997	Diane Grieve / Nancy Carron
1998	Yale Kussin / Lesley Dehaan
1999	Selena Schrier / Angela Will
2000	Johanne Cook / Vicki Egilsson
2001	Deb Tonin / Terry Wanek

22

N. LAKE

TO COUNTY LINE

A few people here will talk but no one seems to know anything. You can tell they are scared. The police have nothing to go on. Talked to an officer who said all those cases are unsolved. There is absolutely no evidence, and no bodies have ever been found. This is likely a phantom attacker of some kind, I am almost certain. The local folklore is similar to Springheel Jack, for example. In London, he terrorized people starting in 1837 . . . strange sightings of a cloaked figure that breathed blue-white fire. It targeted women mostly. Never solved and is still a mystery. Other legends of this type include Nain Rouge, Mothman, and phantom gassers. There are definitely similarities to this Hibbing area phantom.

August 31:
Sam left. I told him that if he was going, it was permanent. I meant it.

November 2:
Mary has been dead for nineteen years. I haven't kept the family together, Mary. I'm sorry. Sam's gone because he's headstrong and because I couldn't make him understand how important this is to all of us. Now Dean tells me he's cut off contact with Sam, and it's killing me. I can't stand the idea of the boys separated. It's one thing for me to take a stand. I'm the father, I have to lay down the law for the family. Maybe that's the Marine in me talking, and maybe it's not the right thing to do all the time, but it's gotten us this far. Now I'm questioning myself. Brothers have to stick together.

2003

January 24:

Dean turns twenty-four today. I was twenty-four when I married his mother. Sorry, kid. Every boy has to cut the apron strings sometime, and for you it's not going to be until we kill off a supernatural entity that seriously needs killing. Then we'll all be free of your mother's ghost. We'll be able to live normal lives. But maybe not. Maybe we've all been hunters too long now.

RP again, 2/1/2003
    Anderson
    Chawla
    Brown
    Clark
    Husband
    McCool
    Raymond

March 20:

Wars and rumors of wars.

Babylonian demon-bowls found facedown, or two glued together. Inside, skull fragments, inscribed eggshells. Bowls

inscribed with Persian charms, ourobouros symbols, bound demons, human figures breaking free of demonic influence. Placed in corners of rooms to trap demons, which were believed to enter at corners of rooms. Could also be used aggressively to guide demons to an adversary. Buried in cemeteries or on the desired target's property.

May 2:

Sam's twentieth birthday. He's in California. Dean and I are packing up to get the hell out of Athens, Ohio, which as of this morning is free and clear of haunted sorority houses. I heard Dean talking about Sam on the phone earlier, but he didn't say anything about the conversation to me. I can't bring it up to Dean, either, especially not the mood he's been in. Usually after a hunt he's on fire, like the killing is a buzz. Today you can't talk to him. If I didn't know better, I'd think it was because of a girl, but we've only been here a couple of weeks. It's not like Dean to fall hard for a girl that fast. He was spending a lot of time with a reporter—think she was a reporter. A looker. Could be anything, though. Hard to tell how he's reacting to Sam going AWOL. Dean's like me. He doesn't talk. He acts. We act.

May 17:

This would have been our twenty-fifth anniversary. That's silver. Associated with the moon in alchemy— maybe that's why silver bullets take out werewolves.

June 13:

Dean heard about a succubus in Brooklyn from Richie. He lit out after it like he bore it a personal grudge. I'm getting more and more sure that he had some kind of girl trouble in Ohio, and every female spirit and demon in North America's going to suffer for it. Just hope he keeps his head.

July 30:

US Route 491 dedicated today. Formerly Route 666, The Devil's Highway. A Navajo medicine man did a ceremony to remove the curse. What do the Navajo care about the Number of the Beast? I'm going to have to go down there again and see. Wonder if the black dogs will give up on the road now. Were they thoughtforms all along, conjured up by all the people who made the connection between the number and the Devil? Was it the name of the road? Or were they real?

October 9:

In Kittanning, Pennsylvania. Poltergeist in a playground built on an old cemetery. Of all the stupid places to put a playground. Sixth or seventh time I've dealt with a poltergeist, enough to know that the psychokinetic theory about girls and puberty is a load of crap. Usually I don't do this, but I've kind of gotten friendly with one of the locals, Jerry Panowski. One of his kids has been targeted a couple of times. For some reason he's easy to talk to. Most of the civilians you meet either don't want to know about the supernatural or blame you for bringing it into their lives once you tell them about it. Jerry's not like that. He understands, I think. Maybe he understands better than I do. Still feel conflicted about Sam. I don't think I did the wrong thing, but I also don't want him out there alone and vulnerable. I've been through Palo Alto half a dozen times in the past year, just to make sure he's okay. I look around, see if there's any sign of anything happening that shouldn't be. He's my son. I can't abandon him. But I also can't go back on what I said. You don't stop loving a kid, but you also can't let love blind you to what's right.

October 27:

Reading around about Samhain, and came across a creature called a puca. It seems to be a distant cousin of the Wild Hunt (also source of the character of Puck?). Quebec version, chasse-galerie, where an unlucky lumberjack gets taken for a ride with the devil on a haunted canoe. Wild Hunt riders recruit accidental viewers to join them, and some can never leave. Often there's a warning not to leave until a certain event has occurred, and the new rider alights to find that centuries have passed. (Typical of visits to the lands of fairies, where time doesn't pass at the same rate . . . see also kitsune stories from Japan.)

Perhaps puca takes riders through time . . . ? To the underworld? Puca said to be able to answer questions, especially on November 1. Would like to know more. Creatures with this kind of ability have *answers,* and *answers* are what I need.

November 2:

Mary has been dead for twenty years. Spent the anniversary at the Winchester Mystery House. After some looking around,

I found a distant family connection. Some great-great-uncle, parallel descent. Genealogy isn't my strong suit. House built after Sarah Winchester got advice from a medium after her husband and daughter died. Medium said the family was haunted because Winchester guns had killed so many people. Sarah had to build a house to distract and trap the spirits, and keep building it until she died. She bought 162 acres, started building in 1882, didn't stop until she died in 1922. Construction was around the clock. House built up to seven stories as of 1906, partially collapsed in the earthquake. Now four stories. Approximately 160 rooms, no one is quite sure. Stairs lead nowhere, doors open onto nothing, hallways wind around into dead ends, secret passages are everywhere. No blueprint or complete plan exists. Sarah would tell the workmen what she wanted done from day to day, sketching partial floor plans on napkins or pieces of paper. Some of those survive.

Number 13 is everywhere. 13 palm trees in front of the house, wall hooks are set in rows of 13, stained-glass windows custom from Tiffany with 13 stones. Chandeliers to fit 13 candles. Spiderweb motif—she thought it was lucky. From story of Saint Felix (lucky)?

525 South Winchester Boulevard. Multiple of 5. 25 times 21. Interesting numbers in there. Sarah chose the address for a reason. Fives are strong, and 21 (3x7) powerful in numerology. Plus the number adds up to 12, and it's symmetrical.

Spotted a valknut, redone as crescent moons. Old Viking symbol related to Odin's powers over the mind, became a symbol of the Trinity in medieval Europe. Also invokes moon symbolism.

This Winchester saga is an interesting flip side to the story of the Colt. Wonder if Samuel Colt was haunted.

2004

January 24:

Dean turns twenty-five today. There was a report on CNN this morning, of a vampire, strigoi, dug up and its heart burned, in Romania less than a month ago.

February 18:

Serious bad mojo, from a houngan in New Iberia: Get bad vinegar, beef gall, filet gumbo with red pepper, and put names written across each other in bottles. Shake the bottle for nine mornings and talk and tell it what you want it to do. To kill the victim, turn it upside down and bury it breast-deep, and he will die.

April 2:

Black Angel, Iowa City. Oakland Cemetery. Pregnant women miscarry, touching can be fatal, walking under wings.

May 2:

Sammy is twenty-one years old today. May he go and get hammered like the college student he is. Was there again last week to keep an eye on him, and he's got a new girlfriend.

May 12:

EXORCISMS WITNESSED 2002-2004

Sheila Farragut

Pedro dos Santos

Philip Kreuzweiler

Ann Stone

Miranda Everett

Gautam Verma

Zeke Halliday

Belinda McAllister

Ken Giang

Deprecatory exorcism. Does not involve a direct command to the possessing demon, so can be performed by laypeople. Can be the Lord's Prayer, but the following is recommended.

Sancte Michael Archangele, defende nos in proelio contra nequitiam et insidias diaboli esto præsidium. Imperet illi Deus, supplices deprecamur: tuque, princeps militiæ cælestis, Satanam aliosque spiritus malignos, qui ad perditionem animarum pervagantur in mundo, divina virtute. In infernum detrude. Amen.

Imprecatory exorcism. Should only be done by a priest if possible. If not, all bets are off. Sign of the cross at X. Supposed to work just as well if not better than the Rituale Romanum.

Exorcizo te, omnis spiritus immunde, in nomine Dei (X) Patris omnipotentis, et in nomine Jesu (X) Christi Filii ejus, Domini et Judicis nostri, et in virtute Spiritus (X) Sancti, ut descedas ab hoc plasmate Dei (name), quod Dominus noster ad templum sanctum

*suum vocare dignatus est, ut fiat templum Dei vivi, et
Spiritus Sanctus habitet in eo. Per eumdem Christum
Dominum nostrum, qui venturus est judicare vivos et
mortuos, et saeculum per ignem.*

Wet fingertips with saliva, and touch the ears and nostrils
of the possessed.

Ephpheta, quod est, Adaperire.
   *In odorem suavitatis. Tu autem effugare, diabole;
appropinquabit enim judicium Dei.*

May 17:

This would have been our twenty-sixth anniversary. Two days
ago, like some awful kind of early present, I got a call from
Bobby. It was a long conversation, and by the end of it, I was a
confirmed believer in demons, because after twenty-one years,
we might just have a real lead on what happened to Mary. All
the things I've seen, and I wrote them off to other kinds of
phenomena . . . *Goddamnit.* I should have been listening all
this time. How much closer would I be? Years of lost time to
make up for. For a while I thought it might have been Lilith,
but now I know better.

   I haven't told Dean yet. Can't take the chance that he'd
try something he's not ready to do. I've already lost Mary, and
Sam. I can't lose Dean too.

October 3:

*Sibly: The form and nature of spirits, say they, are to
be considered according to the force to which each*

caterva doth belong; for some, being altogether of a divine and celestial nature, are not subject to the abominable conjurations and enchantments of vicious men; whilst others, of a diabolical and infernal nature, are not only ready upon all occasions to become subservient to exorcists and magicians, but are ever watching opportunities of exciting evil affections in the mind, and of stirring up the wickedly inclined to the commission of every species of iniquity and vice.

Thus by the instigation of infernal spirits, and their own promptitude, they often terrify men with nocturnal visions; provoke melancholy people to suicide; tempt drunkards and incendiaries to set houses on fire, to burn those who are in them, and allure careless servants and others to sound and incautious sleep; that such unlucky accidents might happen besides innumerable other ways they have of executing the devices of iniquitous spirits through malicious instigations, or secret stratagems, projected for the overthrow and destruction of mortal men; especially when the work to be effected by the devil is too hard for his subtle and spiritual nature to effect, because the same belongs to the outward source or principle to which these dubious spirits more immediately belong.

November 2:

Mary has been dead for twenty-one years. At last I'm getting closer. If it was a demon that killed her, and I think it was, I'm going to nail down which one. Then I'm going to make it suffer.

Sibly on demons:

Their misery is unquestionably great and infinite; but not through the effect of outward flames; for their bodies are capable of piercing through wood and iron, stone, and all terrestrial things. Neither is all the fire or fuel of this world able to torment them; for in a moment they can pierce it through and through.

We'll see.

November 23:

Still tracking the Colt. It's out there somewhere. Word is that a hunter has it, but nobody I know will say who. Someone's hiding it. Why? If I had it, all I'd need is one bullet. A gun that can kill anything . . . one bullet, for the demon that killed Mary. Then I could put down all my guns, and rest.

December 7:

DEMONS WHO USE FIRE, OR
ARE UNDER FIRE SYMBOLS

Amon. Seventh of the ranking spirits of Hell. "Appeareth like a wolf with a serpent's tail, vomiting out of his mouth flames of fire." Nothing about him in Testament of Solomon.

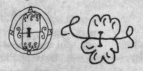

Aim. Twenty-third spirit. Three heads, riding a snake and "carrying a Firebrand in his Hand, wherewith he setteth cities, castles, and great Places, on fire."

Asmoday. Thirty-second spirit. "Sitteth upon an Infernal Dragon," and breathes fire. In Testament of Solomon, he says he can't be forced to tell the truth: "But how shall I answer thee, for thou art a son of man; whereas I was born an angel's seed by a daughter of man, so that no word of our heavenly kind addressed to the earth-born can be overweening." Hates water. According to Weyer, the conjuror's ring can force him to tell the truth.

Amy/Avnas. Fifty-eighth spirit, "appeareth at first in the form of a Flaming Fire." Will take human shape, and disclose secrets and treasures guarded by spirits. Grants familiars.

Haures/Flauros. Sixty-fourth spirit. "He putteth on a human shape with Eyes Flaming and Fiery . . . He destroyeth and burneth up those who be the Enemies of the Exorcist should he so desire it." But also a skilled deceiver if he's not kept within the boundaries of the trap. Will talk of heaven and hell, and of the Fall.

Marchosias. A wolf with griffin's wings, breathes fire, will take human shape. Gives true answers.

Balam. Three heads, burning eyes, rides a bear. Can make things invisible. "Of the order of dominations," according to Weyer.

Allocen. A soldier riding a horse, red-faced and with burning eyes. Will grant familiars.

December 31:

Invocation, from Goetia:

I invoke and conjure you spirit N. & being wth power armed from ye supreame Majesty, I thoroughly command you by Beralanensis, Baldachiensis, Paumachiæ & Apologiæ-Sedes and ye most powerfull princes Genio Liachidi ministers of ye Tartarean seat, Cheefe princes of ye seat of Apologia, in ye Ninth Region; I exorcise & powerfully command you spirit N., in and by him that said ye word, & it was done, and by all ye holy and most glorious Names of ye most holy and true God, and by these his most holy

204

*Names Adonai, El, Elohim, Elohe, Zebeoth, Elion,
Escerchie, Eskerie, Jah, Tetragrammaton Saday That
you forthwth appear and shew yrselves here unto me
before this Circle, in a fair and humane shape, without
any deformity or ugly shew and without delay, doe ye
come, from all parts of ye world to make rationall
answares unto all Things wch I shall ask of you; and
come yee peacebly, visibly and afably without delay,
manifesting wt I desire, being conjured by ye Name
[Names] of ye Eternall liveing and true God Helioren
I conjure you by ye especiall and true Name of your
God that ye owe obediance unto and by ye Name of
yr king, wch beareth rule over you, That forthwith
you come without tarrying, and fullfill my desires,
and command, and persist unto ye End, & according
to my Intentions and I conjure yu by him by whome
all Creatures are obediant unto and by this ineffeble
name Tetragrammaton Jehovah, wch being heard,
ye Elements are overthrown; The aire is shaken, The
sea runneth back, The fire is quenched, The Earth
Trembleth and all ye hosts of Celestialls, Terrestialls
& Infernalls doe Tremble, and are troubled and
confounded together. That you visibly and affebly,
speak unto me with a Clear voice Intelligible, and
without any ambiguity, Therefore come ye in the
Name Adonay Zebeoth; Adonay, Amiorent, com com
why stay you? Hasten: Adonay Saday, the Kinge of
kings commandeth you.*

2005

January 1:

I'm fifty years old, and Mary has been dead for twenty-two of those years. I only knew her for seven. Every year those two numbers get farther apart, because only one of them can change. This year I will find who killed her. This year I will end this and let it all go. Dean turns twenty-six in three weeks. When I was twenty-six, I'd spent two years as a soldier. Dean's been a soldier his whole life. When I was twenty-six, I'd been married for two years and had a toddler. Dean's never been with a woman for more than a couple of weeks at a time. I've prevented him from being a father.

By the time Sammy turns twenty-six, I swear this will be over.

January 5:

Twelfth Night (by the old calendar, when a day started at sunset). The Lord of Misrule is out there somewhere, making peasants out of kings, and behind him the ghosts of Samhain and Saturnalia. I talked to Jim tonight, and the conversation has me spooked. Why? The first time I met the guy, he showed me Mary's spirit and it turned itself into the guise of a hell-hound. Since then, the things we've seen . . . Why should anything I see or hear from Jim spook me after that? Don't know.

When I hung up the phone, I felt like . . . not like someone had walked over my grave, but like I'd just walked over his. I asked him if he was okay, he said he'd never been better. Maybe I'm jumping at shadows, but I'm worried about him.

March 21:

Saturnalia. Agrippa's seals of Saturn:

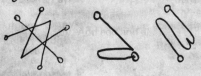

January 24:

Dean turns 26 today. When I was 26, he was a baby. Generations pass. Not handing off the family business to him anytime soon, though. He's got his piece of it, and we're both pulling toward the big goal. I'm starting to tell him more about the demon problem. He doesn't have the head for esoterica that Sam does, but what Dean wants to learn, he learns.

April 7:

To make holy water.

1. Invocation

> EXORCISO te creaturam salis, per Deum vivum + per Deum + verum + per Deum sanctum + per Deum qui te per Elizæum prophetam in aquam mitti jussit, ut sanaretur sterilitas aquæ, ut efficiaris sal exorcisatus in salutem credentium; ut sis omnibus te sumentibus sanitas animæ & corporis, & effugiat at que discedat ab eo loco, qui

aspersus fuerit omnis phantasia & nequitia, vel versutia diabolicæ fraudis, omnisq; spiritus immundus, adjuratus per eum, qui venturus est judicare vivos & mortuos, & sæculum per ignem, amen. Oremus:

Immensam clementiam tuam, omnipotens ceterne Deus, humiliter imploramus, ut hanc creaturam salis, quam in usum generis humani tribuisti, bene + dicere & sancti + ficare tua pietate digneris, ut sit omnibus sumentibus salus mentis & corporis, ut quicquid ex eo tactum fuerit, vel respersum, careat omni immundicia, omniq; impugnatione spiritualis nequitiæ, per Dominum nostrum Jesum Christum filium tuum, qui tecum vivit & regnat in unitate spiritus sancti, Deus per omnia sæcula sæculorum, Amen.

2. Address the following to the water.

Exorciso te creaturam aqua in nomine + patris + & Jesu Christi filii ejus Domini nostri, & in virtute spiritus + sancti + ut fias aqua exorcisata, ad effugandam omnem potestatem inimici, & ipsum inimicum eradicare & explantare valeas, cum angelis suis apostatis, per virtutem ejusdem Domini nostri Jesu Christi, qui venturus est judicare vivos & mortuos, & sæculum per ignem, Amen. Oremus:

Deus, qui ad salutem humani generis maxima qua que sacramenta in aquarum substantia condidisti, adesto propitius invocationibus nostris, & elemento huic multimodis purificationibus præparato, virtutem tuæ bene + didionis infunde, ut creatura tua mysteriis tuis serviens, ad abigendos dæmones, morbosq; pellendos, divinæ gratiæ sumat effectum, ut quicquid in domibus, vel in locis fidelium hæc unda resperserit, careat omni immundicia, liberetur à noxa, non illic resideat spiritus pestilens, non aura corrumpens, discedant omnes insidiæ latentis inimici,

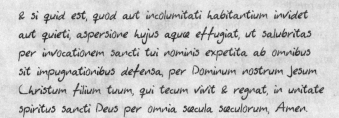

& si quid est, quod aut incolumitati habitantium invidet aut quieti, aspersione hujus aquæ effugiat, ut salubritas per invocationem sancti tui nominis expetita ab omnibus sit impugnationibus defensa, per Dominum nostrum Jesum Christum filium tuum, qui tecum vivit & regnat, in unitate spiritus sancti Deus per omnia sæcula sæculorum, Amen.

3. Say the following as you sprinkle salt into the water, moving your hand in the shape of a cross. Have also heard that you can consecrate with a rosary or cross, or other sacred object.

Commixtio salis & aqua pariter fiat, in nomine patris, & filii, & spiritus sancti, Amen. Dominus vobiscum, Et cum spiritu tuo, Oremus: Deus invictæ virtutis author, & insuperabilis imperii rex, ac semper magnificus triumphator, qui adversæ dominationis vires reprimis, qui inimici rugientis sævitiam superas, qui hostiles nequitias potens expugnas; te Domine trementes & supplices deprecamur ac petimus, ut hanc creaturam salis & aquæ aspicias, benignus illustres, pietatis tuæ rore sancti fices, ubicunq; fuerit aspersa, per invocationem sancti tui nominis, omnis infestatio immundi spiritus abjiciatur, terrórq; venenosi serpentis procul pellatur, & præsentia sancti spiritus nobis misericordiam tuam poscentibus ubiq; adesse dignetur, per Dominum nostrum Jesum Christumfilium tuum, qui tecum vivit & regnat in unitate spiritus sancti Deus per omnia sæcula sæculorum, Amen.

In a pinch, you can skip from the "exorciso te" right to the "per Dominum nostrum Jesum." I tried it. It works.

May 2:

Sammy is twenty-two today. Saw in a Colorado paper that a couple of hikers have gone missing at a place called Blackwater Ridge. Twenty years ago, maybe, eight people were killed up there. Cops called it grizzly attacks.

May 17:

This would have been our twenty-seventh anniversary.

Johann Weyer, student of Agrippa. List of demons:
Bael, Agares, Barbas, Aamon, Barbatos, Buer, Gusoyn, Otis, Bathym, Burson, Abigor, Oray, Malaphar, Foraii, Ipes, Naberus, Caacrinolaas, Zepar, Byleth, Sytry, Paimon, Bune, Fornesu, Ronove, Berith, Astaroth, Forcas, Furrur, Marchocias, Malphas, Vepar, Sabnac, Asmoday, Gaap, Chax, Pucel, Furcas, Murmur, Caym, Raum, Halphas, Focalor, Vine, Bifrons, Gamygyn, Zagam, Orias, Volac, Gomory, Carabia, Amduscias, Andras, Androalphus, Oze, Aym, Orobas, Vapula, Cimeries, Amy, Flauros, Balam, Alocer, Zaleos, Wal, Haagenti, Phoenix, Stolas.

Almost all of these have one thing in common, that once forced into a human shape they will answer questions truthfully. Asmoday an exception? Names mutate in different texts. Some of these demons are probably invention, but the idea of demonic orders is common to all demonologists. Lesser orders are unnamed. Specific instructions on summoning in entry on Bileth. Silver ring mentioned again in Astaroth entry. Sigil of Solomon.

> ... to allaje his courage, let him hold a hazell bat [rod, staff, or stick] in his hand, wherewithall he must reach out toward the east and south, and make a triangle

without besides the circle; but if he hold not out his hand unto him, and he bid him come in, and he still refuse the bond or chain of spirits; let the conjuror proceed to reading, and by and by he will submit him-selfe, and come in, and doo whatsoever the exorcist commandeth him, and he shalbe safe. If Bileth the king be more stubborne, and refuse to enter into the circle at the first call, and the conjuror shew himselfe fear-full, or if he have not the chaine of spirits, certeinelie he will never feare nor regard him after. Also, if the place be unapt for a triangle to be made without the circle, then set there a boll of wine, and the exorcist shall certeinlie knowe when he commeth out of his house, with his fellowes, and that the foresaid Bileth will be his helper, his friend, and obedient unto him when he commeth foorth. And when he commeth, let the exorcist receive him courteouslie, and glorifie him in his pride, and therfore he shall adore him as other kings doo, bicause he saith nothing without other princes. Also, if he be cited by an exorcist, alwaies a silver ring of the middle finger of the left hand must be held against the exorcists face.

Dean: 785-555-0179. As of June 1.

June 19:

<u>Grimorium Verum</u> states three instruments necessary for conjuration: knife, graver, and lancet. Knife and graver should be made on the day and in the hour of Jupiter. The knife should be large enough to decapitate a sacrificial animal—machete-sized.

After completion, recite the following:

I conjure thee, form of the instrument, N., by God the Father Almighty; by the virtue of Heaven and by all the stars which rule; by the virtue of the four elements; by that of all stones, all plants and all animals whatsoever; by the virtue of hailstorms and winds; to receive such virtue herein that we may obtain by thee the perfect issue of all our desires, which also we seek to perform without evil, without deception, by God, the Creator of the Sun and the Angels. Amen.

Then recite the 7 Penitential Psalms: 6, 32, 38, 51, 102, 130. Invoke angels.

The lancet should be created in the day and hour of Mercury, with the same recitation. The knife must be inscribed ELOHIM JITOR.

Reginald Scot has it different.

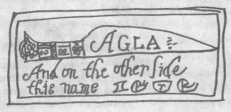

And on the other side this name

July 20:

Bingo. California, New Jersey, Arizona. House fires. In each case, a mother killed and one of the survivors a six-month-old baby. Need to go back and see if there were others on 11/2/83. Either way, this is a hard lead. Looking at locations, survivors, other associated phenomena. Unusual weather, spikes in violence or crime. Any of those things can signify demonic involvement. But the fires are enough. Six of them, within a couple of days, each with a six-month-old involved. You gave yourself away, you bastard.

Almost twenty-two years I've been after you. It's not going to be twenty-three. I'm going to look into your yellow eyes and watch you die.

I want to tell the boys, but won't just yet. Dean might go off half-cocked, and Sammy . . . I was about to write that he wouldn't care. Maybe that's not true. But he might not care enough, and I don't think I could stand knowing that.

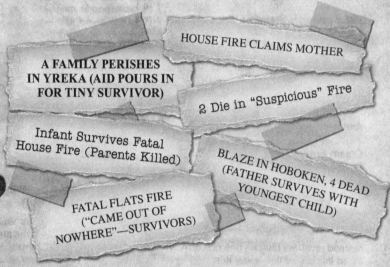

HOUSE FIRE CLAIMS MOTHER

A FAMILY PERISHES IN YREKA (AID POURS IN FOR TINY SURVIVOR)

2 Die in "Suspicious" Fire

Infant Survives Fatal House Fire (Parents Killed)

BLAZE IN HOBOKEN, 4 DEAD (FATHER SURVIVES WITH YOUNGEST CHILD)

FATAL FLATS FIRE ("CAME OUT OF NOWHERE"—SURVIVORS)

August 14:

Last three weeks: Tallahassee, Baton Rouge, Jackson, Birmingham, Atlanta. State records offices all look the same. Then same thing across the Rust Belt: Columbus, Lansing, Harrisburg, Indianapolis. Libraries in every county seat in West Virginia, looking for patterns in the weather records. Feel like I've been everywhere, like I'm living in a Johnny Cash song, only with demonic evil. Come to think of it, "Ghost Riders in the Sky" is a version of the Wild Hunt, isn't it?

September 19:

Autumnal equinox might be the next big breakthrough. Will know in 48 hours. Haven't slept in more than 24 already. Remember old battlefield advice. Eat when you can, sleep when you can, because you never know when the next time will come. Should sleep. Not hungry.

October 3:

Equinox a bust. Dean in New Orleans. Me in Jericho, CA. Trail of the demon that killed Mary cooling a little. People keep going missing from the area right around a bridge here. Started to look around, and it has all the hallmarks of a Woman in White. Almost feel like I should drop this one and keep running the demon down. But to do that, I'd have to let people die. And after all these years, I remember what H told me: A hunter never passes up a hunt. I had to kill him, but he was right about that.

October 4:

La Llorona

Long ago, the story goes, a beautiful Indian princess, Dona Luisa de Loveros, fell in love with a handsome Mexican nobleman named Don Nuno de Montesclaros. The princess loved the nobleman deeply and had two children by him, but Montesclaros refused to marry her. When he finally deserted her and married another woman, Dona Luisa went mad with rage and stabbed her two children. Authorities found her wandering the street, sobbing, her clothes covered in blood. They charged her with infanticide and sent her to the gallows.

Ever since, it is said, the ghost of La Llorona walks the country at night in her bloody dress, crying out for her murdered children. If she finds any child, she's likely to carry it away with her to the nether regions, where her own spirit dwells.

Lovell, Wyoming. Reports of a ghostly woman looking for her children, but will take unlucky passersby instead.

Lampasas, Texas. White girl had a baby by a slave. He was hanged, and she jumped into Sulphur Spring with the baby. Now said to walk near the site of the old slave quarters calling out to him to show him the baby.

Woman in White legends all over the world. Often related to vanishing hitchhiker.

List of recorded Vanishing Hitchhiker incidents:
Ya-Ta-Hey NM (along 666!); Chicago—Resurrection Mary; Greensboro NC; Bluffton IN; along Hwy 365 in Arkansas; Delmar NY; St. Louis; White Rock Lake TX; Tompkinsville KY; Toronto; Spartanburg SC; Berkeley CA; Los Angeles; San Francisco; Clinton Road NJ . . . older stories from all over the world. Korea, China, Japan, Russia, Slovakia, other European countries. Mormon tradition of Nephites.

Interesting variation: Lauderdale, AL, the ghost of a jazz musician in a white zoot suit. If you give him a ride, he will talk about his trumpet before disappearing. Local story is that he was killed while on his way to Florence.

Vanishing hitchhikers often prophesy or tell drivers some secret. Stories like this were especially common in World War II, and in pre-automotive Europe. Related to the myth of the Wandering Jew. Matthew 16:28, Jesus says that some of his witnesses will not die until the Second Coming. Later said to be a shoemaker Cartaphilus, who spurred Jesus along the Via Dolorosa; or Pontius Pilate's footman, Longinus, the Roman soldier who stabbed Jesus with a spear; the servant Malchus, whose ear St. Peter cut off. Goes all the way back to Cain, condemned to wander because of his crime. Later Gypsies said to be descended from the blacksmith who forged the nails for the cross. Various combinations of these stories exist. What they have in common is the theme that as penance, the wanderer must go from place to place testifying about the Second Coming and his own error. Occasionally a female, sometimes Herodias, who laughed at Jesus before the Crucifixion. Wandering Jew appears and disappears without warning.

Always dangerous, because it preys on one of the best human qualities, the impulse to help those in need. The problem with the vanishing hitchhiker is that it never stays vanished. It leaves a token sometimes, which leads the person who offered the ride to try to find it again. Usually that search leads straight to a graveyard, and there's one less Good Samaritan in the world. Some spirits know they can't approach directly, and some just love the game of taking advantage of the better sides of human nature.

October 5:

Glowing eyes: Allocer, Balam, Flauros
Hellhound, puca, leszy, wendigo

Push for
New Generation
of Exorcists

VATICAN RECRUITING EXORCISTS IN U.S.

BENEDICT BEGINS AMERICAN
EXORCIST SEARCH

October 6:

Too much news about exorcists, exorcism lately. It must mean something. Something's on the move, something big.

Azazel: first mentioned as the intended recipient of a scapegoat cast out on Yom Kippur. Leviticus 16:8. Name connotes strength, impudence—cognates have been translated as variants of Angel of Death. Book of Enoch says Azazel was one of the fallen angels who fathered the Nephilim of human women. Enoch also claims Azazel was the first to show men how to make metal weapons and armor. (Also cosmetics, so blame him for that too.) "To him ascribe all sin." Conflict here with the stories of Enoch himself given in the Book of the Watchers. Enoch himself supposed to be an angel descending, to give gifts of knowledge and science. Azazel always associated with goats. Also sometimes with the Lilim.

October 28:

Got a phone call from the roadhouse, and the last piece fell into place. I'm on the trail. Twenty-two years, and I've finally found the sonofabitch. Now I'm going to take him down.

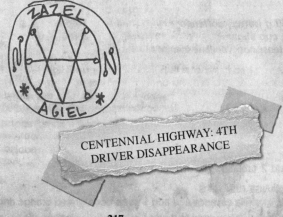

CENTENNIAL HIGHWAY: 4TH
DRIVER DISAPPEARANCE

Acknowledgments

This book would not exist without Eric Kripke, Rebecca Dessertine, Cathryn Humphris, all the writers of *Supernatural*, Chris Cerasi, Kate Nintzel, Dan Panosian, and every scholar and investigator of the occult and strange whose work gave me such a rich field to explore. It also would not exist without the dedicated fans of the show. Thanks to each and every one of you, and to whomever I have inexcusably forgotten.